D1319163

Also by Erle Stanley Gardner
Published by Ballantine Books:

The Case of the
Crooked Candle

Erle Stanley Gardner

BALLANTINE BOOKS • NEW YORK

Copyright © 1944 by Erle Stanley Gardner
Copyright renewed 1972 by Jean Gardner

All rights reserved under International and Pan-American Copyright Conventions. Published in the United States of America by Ballantine Books, a division of Random House, Inc., New York, and simultaneously in Canada by Random House of Canada Limited, Toronto.

ISBN 0-345-34164-3

This edition published by arrangement with William Morrow and Company, Inc.

Manufactured in the United States of America

First Ballantine Books Edition: February 1987
Fourth Printing: April 1992

Cast of Characters

1

Perry Mason pushed open the door of his private office, smiled at Della Street who was dusting the corners of his desk with secretarial solicitude.

"Good morning, Chief," she said.

Mason gravely deposited his hat in the hat closet, walked over to the desk and looked down at the mail, neatly arranged in three piles, on the first of which was a placard, *"Should be read—needs no answer."* The second pile was labeled, *"Must be read, but can be answered without necessity of your dictation."* The third pile consisted of some half dozen letters which had been marked, *"Must be read and answered by you personally."*

Della Street entered her secretarial office which adjoined that of Perry Mason's. She dropped the dust cloth in a drawer in her desk, returned to Mason's office, and propping her shorthand notebook over her crossed knee, held a pencil poised, waiting for Mason to begin dictating.

Mason started with the pile of letters demanding his personal attention, read through the first one, paused to look out of the window, and then, with his eyes fastened upon the Southern California cloudless sky, said abruptly, "It's Friday, Della."

Della nodded, held her pencil in readiness.

"Why," Mason asked abruptly, "do they invariably execute murderers on Friday?"

"Probably because it's considered unlucky to start a journey on Friday," Della said.

"Exactly," Mason announced. "It's a barbarous custom. We should give the murderer a chance to start the next world with a clean slate."

"Other people die on Fridays just the same as any other day," Della observed. "Why should murderers be exempt?"

Mason lowered his eyes from the window to look at her. "Della, you are fast becoming a realist. And has it ever occurred to you that we may get in a rut?"

"Getting in a rut around *this* office is the last thing that would ever enter my mind," Della said with feeling.

Mason indicated the suite of offices on the other side of the closed doors which led to the law library and the reception room. "Beyond those doors, Della, is a hum of routine activity. Gertie at the switchboard putting through calls, getting the names, addresses and occupations of clients who come in. In an office which opens from the reception room, Jackson is sitting in beetle-browed efficiency. There's something for you to consider, Della, the case of Jackson—a man who has become so steeped in legalistic lore that a *'negative pregnant'* elicits greater emotional response than a thirteen-inning baseball game. His life has been so ordered by the conventional rules of law that he simply can't adjust himself to anything new. He . . ."

Knuckles tapped on the door from the law library.

Mason said to Della, "This will be Exhibit A in making my point—Jackson himself. Come in!"

Jackson pushed the door open. His spare frame seemed somewhat bowed under the weight of the ponderous dignity which it carried about. His face, thin and sharp, cast in lines of austere concentration, showed a long nose, a thin determined mouth which was beginning to turn sharply down at the corners. Deep calipers had etched themselves down from the nostrils, but there was no

2

frown in the forehead, only the calm of complete tranquillity. Jackson's conviction that everything must be done according to law was supplemented by an assurance that he knew exactly what the law was, which gave him an omnipotent serenity.

Jackson, too engrossed with his legal problem to waste time in "Good mornings," said, "I have a *very* perplexing case. I hardly know whether I'm justified in going ahead. A big truck owned by the Skinner Hills Karakul Company transporting some Karakul fur sheep, came to a sudden stop. The driver failed to give any signal. A car operated by Arthur Bickler, who is asking us to represent him, ran into the rear end of the truck and was rather seriously damaged."

"Anyone in the car with him?"

"Yes, his wife, Sarah Bickler."

Mason, grinning, said, "I suppose the truck driver says he gave a signal; that he was going to stop; that he was looking in his rearview mirror and saw this car approaching rapidly; that he could see the man was talking to the woman and wasn't even watching the road; that he blew his horn three times, waved his hand frantically, then switched on and off his rear lights, trying to attract the man's attention as he slowed down."

Jackson didn't even smile. He peered in owlish concentration through his glasses as he consulted his notes. "No. The truck driver insists that he gave a signal and that he saw the car approaching rapidly in his rearview mirror; that the car made no attempt to stop, but slammed into the rear of his truck. He doesn't say anything about noticing that the man at the wheel of the sedan wasn't watching the road."

Mason gave Della Street an amused glance. "Probably an inexperienced truck driver."

"A most peculiar situation thereupon developed," Jackson went on. "Arthur Bickler got out of the sedan. The truck driver emerged from behind the wheel of the truck.

3

There was the usual exchange of comment, of recriminations and assertions. Then Arthur Bickler took a pencil from his pocket and wrote down the name, "Skinner Hills Karakul Company," which was on a placard fastened to the side of the truck. No one made any objection."

"Why should they?" Mason asked.

Jackson blinked thoughtfully. "That," he said, "is the peculiar part of it. Mr. Bickler then went around to the rear of the truck and wrote down the license number of the truck. No sooner had he done this than the truck driver reached out, said, 'Naughty, naughty!' took Bickler's pencil and notebook away and dropped both of them in his pocket, then climbed back in his truck and drove away."

"Any physical injuries?" Mason asked.

"Mrs. Bickler sustained a nerve shock."

"Any listing in the phone book of Skinner Hills Karakul Company?"

"No. What's more they haven't filed any declaration of firm name, nor of fictitious name."

"All right," Mason said, "get Paul Drake on the job. There are only a few places that sell Karakul breeding stock. Drake can get in touch with those places and see if they have recently sold sheep for delivery in the Skinner Hills district; or if they know anything about the Skinner Hills Karakul Company. It shouldn't be hard to get a lead on them."

"We are confronted in this case by all the uncertainties of the average accident case," Jackson pointed out. "Our client may be without a remedy under the doctrine of 'Last Clear Chance.' Then there is also the question of contributory negligence. I am somewhat dubious . . ."

"Don't let yourself get that way," Mason interrupted. "A dubious lawyer isn't worth a damn to himself or to his client. If you think we have a chance, go to it."

"Very well. Since there is the question of advancing

4

money for an investigation, I thought I should have your permission before incurring the expense."

"You have it," Mason said.

Jackson closed the door, and Mason looked at Della Street with twinkling eyes. "You must admit Jackson's a bit conservative."

Della said demurely, "Aren't *all* lawyers?"

Mason raised his eyebrows and Della added hastily, "An impulsive lawyer might be dangerous."

"The trouble," Mason said, "is that cautious lawyers get in a rut. Now take Jackson. His mind is occupied with demurrers, with pleas in confession-and-avoidance. He has no use for the extemporaneous. He has thwarted all impulses. He never trusts his own ideas. Unless he can find a case which is 'on all fours' he's afraid even to think. When he married, he married a widow. He doubtless could make no romantic approach to a woman until he had evidence that previous romantic activities had been established, thereby having the assurance of precedent and . . ."

Mason's telephone rang. Mason nodded to Della, and she answered it, turned to Mason and said, "Gertie wants to know if you will accept a call from Mr. Sticklan of the firm of Sticklan, Crowe & Ross. He insists on talking with you personally."

Mason reached for the telephone. "Tell Gertie to put him on—Hello."

"C. V. Sticklan, Mr. Mason, of Sticklan, Crowe & Ross."

"Yes, Mr. Sticklan."

"Are you representing a client by the name of Bickler—Arthur Bickler? An auto accident case?"

"Yes."

"What," Sticklan asked, "would your clients want by way of settlement?"

"How much are you willing to pay?"

Sticklan's voice was cautious. "For a complete release

5

from all parties concerned, my clients *might* go as high as three hundred dollars."

"You're representing the Skinner Hills Karakul Company?"

"Yes."

"I'll call you back."

"Call me as soon as you can," Sticklan said. "My client is anxious to get the matter disposed of."

Mason hung up the phone, grinned at Della Street and said, "Things are looking up, Della. Ask Jackson to come in here."

A few moments later, Della Street was back with Jackson in tow.

"The Bicklers still in your office?" Mason asked.

"Yes."

"How much do they want for complete settlement?"

"I haven't discussed that. He feels his automobile was damaged to the extent of two hundred and fifty dollars."

"How much was it actually damaged?"

"Well," Jackson said dubiously, "if you could get the parts, the damage might not be so great. But then, of course—well, in any event, two hundred and fifty dollars is what he *wants*."

"And Mrs. Bickler, what does she want for her nervous shock?"

"She's talking about five hundred dollars."

"They'd settle for seven hundred and fifty?"

"Oh, unquestionably. Five hundred would be considered a good settlement."

"Go see them," Mason said. "Find out if five hundred is all right."

Jackson was gone for less than two minutes. "Five hundred dollars for a cash settlement will be very acceptable," he said.

Mason's eyes were twinkling. He picked up the telephone, said to Gertie, "Get me C. V. Sticklan, of Sticklan, Crowe & Ross, on the telephone."

A few moments later when he had Sticklan on the telephone Mason said, "I find the situation a little more serious than I had at first suspected. Not only is there a property damage, but Mrs. Bickler suffered a severe nervous shock and . . ."

"How much?" Sticklan interrupted.

"Moreover," Mason went on, "there was a highhanded disregard of the rights of our client, the larceny of . . ."

"How much?"

"Twenty-five hundred dollars."

"What!" Sticklan shouted.

"You heard me," Mason said. "Next time, don't interrupt me when I'm listing a client's grievances."

"That's absurd. That's outrageous. That's out of all reason."

"Okay," Mason said. "Have it your own way," and promptly hung up the telephone.

Jackson's eyes were wide. "What," he asked, "is the idea?"

Mason placed his watch on the desk. "Give him five minutes. That will give him an opportunity to communicate with his client and make me a counter offer."

"But how did these lawyers know we were handling the case?"

"Probably tried to reach the Bicklers, found out they were at a lawyer's office, asked the neighbors. . . . How the devil do *I* know, Jackson? The point is they're in a frenzy to get it cleaned up."

Mason watched the second hand on his watch. The telephone rang.

"Two minutes and ten seconds," Mason said cheerfully, and picked up the telephone.

"Mr. Mason," Sticklan said, his voice harsh with anxiety, "I've communicated with my clients. They feel that the demands of your clients are out of all reason."

"All right," Mason said cheerfully, "we'll file suit and see how a jury feels about it. We . . ."

"But my clients," Sticklan interrupted hastily, "are prepared to offer twelve hundred and fifty dollars for a complete settlement."

"No soap," Mason announced.

"Look here," Sticklan pleaded. "In order to get the matter disposed of, *I'll* take the responsibility of asking them to put on another two hundred and fifty dollars and make it a total of fifteen hundred dollars."

Mason said, "Mrs. Bickler sustained a severe nervous shock."

"Nothing that a little money won't cure, I trust," Sticklan said sarcastically.

"That's doing my client an injustice," Mason reproached. "Tell you what I'll do, Sticklan. Tell your clients that if they'll pay two thousand dollars within the next hour, we'll sign a settlement. How soon will you let me know?"

"Just a moment," Sticklan said. "Hold the phone."

Mason heard the faint murmur of voices, then Sticklan was back on the line. "Very well, Mr. Mason, one of my men will be over at your office with a certified check within thirty minutes. Have your clients wait there, please. There'll be a complete release for them to sign. We'll want the release signed in front of a notary."

Mason grinned at Jackson as he hung up. "Probably," he announced, "my conscience should bother me, Jackson, but it doesn't."

Jackson's forehead was furrowed. "I don't know how you do it. I'd have settled for five hundred," he said glumly. "I lived a hundred years in that two minutes and ten seconds."

Mason said, "Just a moment before you go, Jackson. I seem to recall having heard something about the Skinner Hills recently. Don't we have a matter in the office pertaining to property in that district?"

Jackson shook his head, then suddenly caught himself and said, "Wait a minute! There's that Kingman case."

8

"Just what is the Kingman case?" Mason asked.

"Remember you received a letter from Adelaide Kingman that you turned over to me? I corresponded with her and advised bringing suit to quiet title. But she didn't feel that she had the money to go ahead with a lawsuit, so I guess the matter has been virtually dropped."

"Tell me more about it," Mason said.

Jackson cleared his throat with the somewhat pompous formality which was a characteristic preliminary of all his legal utterances. "Adelaide Kingman has the record title to a tract of land in the Skinner Hills district, a piece covering eighty acres of hillside. She executed a contract of sale with a sheepherder named Frank Palermo. The contract price was, I believe, around five hundred dollars. The land is virtually valueless except for a very few acres which are suitable for sheep grazing. Palermo didn't pay the contract price, but insists that he is entitled to the property because of some financial failure on her part. He's been in possession for several years and has had the property assessed to him and paid the taxes. He claims to have a title by adverse possession. Apparently he's one of those smart, cunning, grasping, aggressive individuals who try to chisel at every opportunity."

"And Adelaide Kingman wouldn't go ahead with a quiet title action?" Mason asked.

"No. She sustained an accident—a broken leg. I understand she's in a ward in a San Francisco hospital. She is sixty-five years old and virtually without funds. She felt that, under the circumstances, she couldn't afford to start suit or advance the preliminary costs."

Mason said, "Sit down, Jackson. Let's do a little thinking."

Jackson seated himself across the desk.

Mason asked, "Why do you suppose this Skinner Hills Karakul Fur Company made a settlement in the way they did, and at the time they did?"

"Doubtless they were afraid to go to court when they

9

heard of the manner in which the truck driver had violently taken possession of Arthur Bickler's notebook and pencil."

Mason shook his head. "There was an automobile accident," he said. "A report doubtless was made. Nothing was done until after ten o'clock this morning. Get that point fixed definitely in your mind, Jackson. It was after ten o'clock."

"What does that have to do with it?" Jackson asked.

Mason said, "That's something for us to consider. Ten o'clock is significant in what way?"

"It's the time the banks open?" Della Street suggested.

"And the time that big executives come to work," Mason added. "So let's suppose that this report of the accident was handed to an underling, who in turn placed it on the desk of a big executive at ten o'clock this morning. The big executive tried to get in touch with Bickler by rushing an adjuster out to his house. The man found that Bickler had gone to see an attorney. Probably one of the neighbors told him the name of the attorney. Thereupon, this big executive, whoever he was, rings up his attorneys and advises them to settle the case no matter what it costs. Why?"

Jackson shook his head. "I don't get it."

Mason said, "I *think* I get it. Della, get Paul Drake at the Drake Detective Agency. Tell him to investigate the Skinner Hills Karakul Company; to get in touch with breeders of Karakul fur sheep, and find out to whom sales have been made. Have him look up everything he can in connection with the Skinner Hills Karakul Company and, above all, when that release comes over for Bickler to sign, see if we can't get Bickler's notebook back. Then get the license number of the truck in which the sheep were being transported. I think you'll find that the license number of that truck is the key factor in the whole situation."

Jackson seemed somewhat dazed. "I am free to confess," he announced, "that I fail to follow your reasoning processes, Mr. Mason."

"Never mind trying," Mason said, and added with a grin, "I'm not even certain I'm following what you would refer to as reasoning processes. I'm playing hunches. Ring up Adelaide Kingman, tell her not to make any settlement of any sort, or sign anything until we tell her, and tell her to refer any inquiries to us. Also advise her that we're taking her out of the ward and putting her in a private room with special nurses. Then see that the best bone specialist in San Francisco is called into consultation tomorrow morning."

Jackson's eyes showed bewildered astonishment. "And who foots the bill?" he asked.

"We do," Mason said.

2

The next morning Paul Drake, long, lean, lanky and moving with double-jointed ease, jackknifed himself into his favorite crossways position in the big overstuffed leather chair and grinned at Perry Mason. "Why the sudden interest in Karakul fur, Perry?"

"I don't know, I might want to buy a fur coat. What have you found out, Paul?"

Drake said, "That Karakul fur company is like the rabbit in a magician's hat—now you see it, and now you don't. It's right out in the open, and yet it isn't in the open. It's bought up a lot of property in the Skinner Hills district."

"For what purpose?"

"For the raising of Karakul fur sheep."

"Why the Skinner Hills?" Mason asked.

"A staff of glib-tongued realtors have been explaining that. It has *just* the right amount of sunlight, *just* the proper amount of rainfall and has a certain percentage of minerals in the soil that are highly advantageous."

"Who are back of the glib-tongued salesmen?" Mason asked.

"Chap by the name of Fred Milfield seems to be the main one. He lives at 2291 West Narlian Avenue—that's an apartment house. He's married. Wife is Daphne Milfield. They both came from Nevada with a background around Las Vegas."

12

"Any more salesmen?" Mason asked.

"Man named Harry Van Nuys, thirty-five, thin, slim waisted, pale skinned, eyes dark, rather insolent, also with a background of Las Vegas, Nevada, living in room 618 at the Hotel Cornish, if you can ever find him. My men haven't been able to so far."

"How about Milfield?"

"We haven't been in touch with him directly, just crossed his back trail. About forty-five, self-satisfied, paunchy, blond hair—what there is of it, wide blue eyes that are inclined to pop out a bit, giving him an expression of extreme candor. They've been going through that Skinner Hills district like a house afire."

"Buying or leasing?"

"Buying and contracting."

"Why do you say that the company is like a rabbit in a magician's hat, Paul?"

"There's someone back of it that you can't smoke out. A man no one ever sees, a man whom no one knows."

"How do you know?"

"Just various little things."

"That," Mason announced, "is the man I want."

"He's going to be hard to find. I can tell you this much: Milfield put through a deal that required a lot of cash in a hurry. He and the man with whom he was dealing went to a bank in Bakersfield. Milfield pulled a blank check from his pocket, filled it in for the amount of money he needed and shoved it through the window. There was a little hub-bub about it, and the deal was stalled along while the teller went into the manager's office and was closeted with him just about long enough for a call to have been put through to Los Angeles. The signature on the check that Milfield filled out was in a very peculiar vertical handwriting. The man who was waiting to get the money couldn't see what the first name of the signature was, but he says the last name was Burbank. Does that mean anything to you?"

13

"Not a damn thing," Mason said, "except that Burbank is pretty apt to be the man I want."

"Just what do you want with him, Perry?"

"Specifically, I want to sell him eighty acres of sheep land for about a hundred thousand bucks."

"What's the idea?" Drake asked.

"Did you smell anything while you were making this investigation, Paul?"

"What do you mean?"

Mason sniffed the air and said, "I can smell it."

"What?"

"Oil."

Drake whistled.

"What," Mason asked, "have they been paying for the land?"

"No more than they had to. Understand, Perry, this is Saturday noon. I've been working on the thing for only a little more than twenty-four hours. Even with the number of men I've been able to put on the job, I've had to hit the high spots. The ways things are now, you can't . . ."

"I know," Mason interrupted sympathetically, "but I'm working against time myself. Once they get that property pretty well sewed up, they won't be so gun shy. While they're getting it sewed up, anyone who can walk in and call the turn can write his own ticket. I want to write my own ticket—on behalf of a woman named Adelaide Kingman who is lying in a San Francisco hospital with a broken leg, and the conviction that she hasn't got a cent in the world."

"Well," Drake said, "you can get either Milfield or Van Nuys . . ."

don't want them," Mason said. "I want this man who's back of the whole business, the mysterious somebody who came into his office at ten o'clock yesterday morning, found out that a man by the name of Bickler had taken down the license number of one of his trucks

14

and worked himself into such a dither over that fact that he rang up his attorneys and told them to settle with Bickler no matter what Bickler wanted. He's the man I can do business with."

"Can't you get anything from the license number of the truck?" Drake asked.

Mason laughed. "Fat chance. They gave Bickler back his notebook and his pencil, all right. It was a loose leaf notebook. One of the pages is gone. You can't prove anything. It's just one of those things. Okay, they're working fast, and I'm going to work fast myself."

"Well," Drake said, "that's everything I've got to date, Perry. My men are still working on it, but the only leads we can get point to Milfield and Van Nuys, and we can't actually *find* either one of them."

Mason looked at his watch, then drummed his fingertips on the edge of his desk, "They're paying sheep land prices?" he asked.

"That's all they're paying on the record," Drake said, "but the really smart guys who held out apparently got a spot cash bonus handed to them which doesn't show on any of the papers. You can't prove it. You can guess at it. Have a heart, Perry. Give me until Monday afternoon and I'll have the whole pattern laid out for you and . . ."

"Monday afternoon may be too late," Mason said. "I'm going to see Daphne Milfield. What have your men found out about her?"

"Not a damned thing," Drake said, "except that she's Fred Milfield's wife, and that she lives at this apartment house on West Narlian Avenue."

Mason nodded to Della Street, "Stick around for half an hour," he said. "It's probably a wild goose chase, but anyway it's a chance."

3

∎

The West Narlian Avenue address was an apartment house of the better class. Evidently an attempt had been made to create an atmosphere of exclusive dignity, and the man at the desk in the lobby seemed to be at some pains to impress upon Perry Mason the fact that it was only owing to the labor shortage that the services of the switchboard operator had been discontinued.

"Mr. Fred Milfield," he repeated after Mason. "And your name, please?"

"Mason."

"He is expecting you, Mr. Mason?"

"No."

"Just a moment, please—we've had so much trouble keeping switchboard operators that we're having to get along as best we can. Excuse me a moment, please."

He moved over to a secretarial chair in front of the switchboard, plugged in a line and spoke into a shielded mouthpiece so that it was impossible for Mason to hear what he said.

After a few moments he turned back to Mason and said, "Mr. Milfield isn't in. He isn't expected until late this evening."

"Mrs. Milfield there?" Mason asked carelessly.

The man turned once more to the telephone, then, after a brief conversation, turned back again. "She doesn't place you, Mr. Mason."

Mason said, "Tell her I called to discuss the Karakul sheep business."

The clerk seemed mystified, but passed on the message. "She'll see you. It's apartment Fourteen B. You may go right up."

A Negro in blue livery with a touch of gold braid operated the elevator with the unsure manner that indicated that he was a beginner.

The elevator stopped a good three inches short of the floor, then as the boy tried to compensate for that error, he overshot the mark by some five inches, dropped the cage back so that it was in a worse position than when he had started, grinned, brought it up to within a couple of inches of the floor and opened the door.

"Watch your step," he cautioned.

"You may have something there," Mason told him, and walked out of the cage and down the corridor while the perplexed lad in the elevator was puzzling over his comment.

Mason pushed on the button at Fourteen B, and a few seconds later the door was opened by a woman somewhere in the thirties. She had watched her figure, she had a well-groomed appearance, and her face showed alert awareness of life, but there was a peculiarly puffy look about the eyes.

"Yes?" she asked, standing in the doorway. "You wanted to ask me something about Karakul fur?"

"Yes."

"Can't you tell me what it is, please? My husband isn't here at the moment."

Mason once more glanced up and down the corridor.

"I'll go down to the lobby with you," Mrs. Milfield said with cool detachment; then hesitated, apparently thinking of something which made her change her mind. "Oh well, perhaps you'd better come in."

Mason followed her into a well-furnished apartment. Momentarily, she turned so that the light from a south

17

window struck her face, and Mason saw the peculiar appearance of her eyes was due to the fact that she had been crying. The swollen appearance around the lids and underneath the eyes was unmistakable. This had been no sudden burst of tears over some petty annoyance, but had been a long drawn-out crying spell.

She seemed conscious at once of Mason's deduction, and promptly seated herself with her back to the window. Indicating a chair which faced her, she said to Mason, "Won't you sit down?"

Mason sat down facing the light. He took a cardcase from his pocket. "I'm an attorney."

She took the card he handed her. "Oh yes, I've heard of you. I thought you handled murder cases."

"All sorts of trial work," he told her. "My office carries on a general practice."

"And may I ask why you're interesting yourself in Karakul sheep?"

Mason said, "I have a client who wants money."

She smiled. "Don't all clients want money?"

"Most of them do. This one really needs it. I'm going to get it for her."

"That's nice of you. Does it concern my husband?"

"It concerns his Karakul sheep business."

"Can you be more specific?"

"My client's name is Kingman, Adelaide Kingman."

"I'm afraid the name means nothing to me. You see I don't know the details of my husband's business."

"It is very important that I see him at once."

"I'm afraid he won't be available until the first of the week, Mr. Mason."

"Can you tell me how I can get in touch with him?"

"No. I'm afraid not."

"Can you get in touch with him—immediately?"

She thought that over, then said, "Not immediately."

Mason said, "As soon as you can reach him, tell him that I have a very sensitive nose and that I've been smelling around the Skinner Hills district, that what I smell doesn't smell like Karakul fur. Can you remember that?"

"Why—I guess so. What a strange message, Mr. Mason!"

"And tell him that if necessary I can have my client talk with her neighbors, but that it might be better if she didn't—better for him. And remember to tell him the name is Adelaide Kingman."

She smiled. "I'll tell him."

Mason said, "It's important he understands my position and that he gets my message at once."

"Very well."

"You'll try to see that he gets it?"

"Mr. Mason, you wouldn't try to take advantage of me by reading my facial expressions, would you? I'm torn between a desire to be polite, and the urge to keep what is known as a poker face."

She smiled at him and Mason saw that she had forgotten for the moment that her face showed the ravages of a crying spell.

Mason bowed. "I certainly wouldn't even try to get you to betray your husband's business secrets, Mrs. Milfield," he assured her, "but I *do* want to impress upon your mind the necessity of getting my message to your husband at once."

Abruptly she said, "Mr. Mason, I'm going to confide in you. I need you. I—I'm going to tell you something." She paused, seemed to brace herself, inhaled a deep breath as one does who is starting a rush of words.

The ringing of the telephone bell froze the first of those words on her lips. She looked at the instrument with definite annoyance.

Her embarrassment was sufficiently evident so Mason couldn't resist saying, "Perhaps that's your husband now."

She bit at her lip, moved uneasily in her chair. The telephone rang once more.

Mason sat quietly waiting, saying nothing, putting the next move definitely up to her.

Her hesitancy became the more marked as she quite apparently debated with herself whether it would be more awkward to accept what was very evidently an unwelcome call in Mason's presence, or betray herself by refusing to answer the telephone while he was there.

Abruptly she snapped, "Excuse me," and picked up the receiver. Her face, turned now so that the light shone on her profile, was a graven mask.

"Yes?" she asked in the carefully modulated voice of one who is guarding against betraying her thoughts by any vocal inflection.

Mason watched her face, saw it change into puzzled perplexity. "Why no, I don't know a Mr. Tragg. . . . *Lieutenant* Tragg. No I don't. . . . Oh, I see. . . . Tell him my husband won't be back until sometime late this evening. . . . He does? I can't. . . . He is . . . ? Oh!"

She dropped the receiver back into place, said angrily to Mason, "The nerve of the man! He's on his way up here. I simply won't answer the bell."

"Wait a minute," Mason said rapidly. "Do you know who Lieutenant Tragg is?"

"I suppose he's some lonely soldier who . . ."

"Lieutenant Tragg," Mason said, "is not a soldier. He's a lieutenant of police. He's from headquarters and connected with the homicide squad. I don't know why you've been crying, Mrs. Milfield, but Lieutenant Tragg doesn't mix around with petty crime. If you're connected with a homicide, you'd better start thinking—*and think fast!*"

She turned to him and he saw the blank dismay in her eyes.

Mason regarded her steadily. "Whom do you know that's been murdered?"

"Good heavens! No one, except perhaps my . . ."

"Go on," Mason prompted as she checked herself in mid-sentence.

20

"No. No! No one."

"You said 'my' and then stopped," Mason reminded her. "That possessive pronoun is a giveaway. Were you going to say 'my husband'?"

"Heavens no! Whatever gave you that idea? What are you trying to do—put words in my mouth?"

"Why have you been crying?" Mason asked.

"Who said I'd been crying?"

"Look. We haven't all day to talk things over. Incidentally, if anything *has* happened to your husband, and Tragg should find me here, it would put you in a spot. You'd never be able to explain to him that I hadn't called on you at your request. Is there a back way out?"

"No."

"Got any onions in the house?"

Her eyes widened with perplexity, "Onions! What do onions have to do with it?"

Mason said, "I'm going to duck into the pantry. Don't tell Tragg I'm here. Don't let him know you know me. Put some onions in the sink. Put on an apron. When he rings the bell, go to the door with a knife in your hand, and tell him you were just peeling some onions—that is, if you want to save yourself a lot of trouble. That's just a gratuitous tip from a casual acquaintance. You . . ."

The buzzer on the doorbell sounded explosively.

Mason picked up his hat, grabbed Mrs. Milfield around the waist, rushed her back to the kitchen. "Where's an apron?"

"Hanging up—there."

Mason put the loop of the apron over her head, hastily knotted it behind her waist.

"Get the onions. It's the only way you can account for those swollen eyes."

She opened a bin, and Mason dumped onions into the sink.

The buzzer sounded again—a prolonged, harsh, strident summons.

Mason pulled open a drawer, found kitchen knives, took one out, sliced an onion in half, grabbed Mrs. Milfield's right hand, smeared onion on it, said, "All right, go to the door. Be careful what you say. Remember to tell him you were just fixing onions, and above all, don't say anything about my having been here. Good luck!"

Mason patted her shoulder, gave her a gentle push toward the door, just as Lieutenant Tragg rang the bell for the third time.

Mason moved silently across the kitchen, opened the door of the pantry, found a stool and settled himself as comfortably as he could.

He heard the front door open, heard the sound of voices in the first tentative preliminaries of conversation, heard the door close and the voices become louder and the words more rapid. He couldn't distinguish their words, but he could hear the rumble of Lieutenant Tragg's voice, and the higher pitched notes of Mrs. Milfield's answers.

Abruptly Mason heard Mrs. Milfield give a half suppressed scream; then there were several moments of silence—a silence which was eventually broken once more by the insistent murmur of Lieutenant Tragg's voice.

After that, the conversation was lowered, finally died away altogether.

Mason impatiently glanced at his wrist watch, opened the pantry door an inch and listened.

He could hear people moving around in the front room. He heard a door open and close, and then once more the sound of Tragg's voice. He was asking some question about shoes.

Mason gently closed the pantry door, went back to his position on the stool, let his eyes rove around in an appraisal of the food on the pantry shelves, and eventually yielded to the temptation of a carton of crisp soda crackers.

The lawyer raised the lid, thrust in his hand and, locking his heels in the rungs of the stool, started munching soda crackers.

A few moments later he spied a jar of peanut butter. He spread the creamy, golden mixture on crackers with his pocket knife, and was fairly well covered with crumbs by the time the pantry door was jerked open.

Mason didn't glance up until he had finished spreading peanut butter on the soda cracker he was holding.

Lieutenant Tragg said, "It's okay, Mason. You can come out now."

"Thanks," Mason said nonchalantly, "I've been wanting a glass of milk."

"It's in the icebox," Mrs. Milfield said. "I'll get it for you." Her voice was syrup smooth.

Tragg looked Mason over and suddenly burst out laughing. "What," he asked, "was the idea?"

Mason said, "I was just giving you a break, Lieutenant."

"Giving *me* a break!" Tragg exclaimed.

"That's right."

"I don't get you."

Mason said, "I was calling on Mrs. Milfield in connection with a matter of business. I didn't know what your business was, but I realized that if you found me here, it would put her in an embarrassing position and start you off on a wrong scent. So I decided to keep out of the way until after you had left."

Mrs. Milfield said, "Here's the milk, Mr. Mason."

Mason took the quart bottle of milk over to the drainboard of the sink. Mrs. Milfield gave him a glass. Mason poured out a glass of milk and grinned at Lieutenant Tragg over the rim.

"Here's looking at you, Lieutenant."

Tragg said, "You didn't think you were really going to slip this one over on me, did you, Mason?"

Mason, his mouth full of crackers, managed to enunciate clearly enough to be understood. "Certainly not. I

23

was merely trying to keep you from slipping one over on yourself. Who's the victim this time, Lieutenant?"

"What makes you think there is a victim?"

"Isn't this a professional call?"

"Let's talk about *your* call, first."

Mason grinned. "I have nothing to conceal. I just dropped in for lunch."

Tragg said irritably, "This isn't getting us anywhere, Mason."

"It's getting me a darn good lunch. Very nice peanut butter, Mrs. Milfield. Permit me to compliment you on it."

"Thank you."

Tragg said, "All right, wise guy. Mrs. Milfield's husband has been murdered."

"Too bad," Mason mumbled, his mouth full of cracker.

"I don't suppose *you* know anything about it," Tragg said.

"Only what you've told me."

Tragg looked at the onions in the sink.

"These the onions you were peeling?" he asked Mrs. Milfield.

"Yes."

"Where are the peeled ones?"

"I . . . I had just started when you rang the doorbell."

Tragg said, "Humph!" and after a moment, shot Mason a suspicious glance.

"Where was her husband murdered?" Mason asked conversationally, taking two or three swallows of milk.

Tragg grinned. "By a technicality, Mason, it's within the city limits of Los Angeles."

"Makes it nice," Mason observed. "Gives you something to do. Who did it?"

"We don't know."

"Sounds interesting," Mason commented.

Tragg said nothing.

"How did you know I was here?" Mason asked abruptly.

"I told him you were," Mrs. Milfield said.

"Why?" Mason asked, pouring himself another glass of milk.

Tragg said, "You're making me hungry, Mason."

"Help yourself," Mason told him cordially. "It's one of the police prerogatives, you know. Why did you tell him, Mrs. Milfield?"

"I thought I'd better, after I found out what it was all about. I didn't want to be placed in a false light."

"Certainly not," Mason observed, washing his hands at the tap in the kitchen sink, and tearing off a paper towel from the roll above the drainboard.

"I explained to Lieutenant Tragg," she went on, "that you were calling on me in connection with another matter —something that had to do with my husband's business; and that when you heard Tragg was here, you thought it would be better if he didn't find you."

Tragg grinned. "You don't need to coach *him,* Mrs. Milfield. He knows all the lines, even yours."

Mason shook his head, dolefully. "I told you so, Mrs. Milfield. He doesn't trust me. Well, I'll be on my way. I'm sorry about your husband. I don't suppose Lieutenant Tragg gave you any particulars?"

She said, "Why yes. He gave me all the details. It seems that . . ."

"Hold it!" Tragg interrupted sharply. "What I told you wasn't to be passed on."

She lapsed into silence.

Tragg moved over to look at the onions in the sink. He was frowning thoughtfully.

Mason said, "Well, I'm on my way. My sincere sympathies, Mrs. Milfield."

"Thank you." She turned to Lieutenant Tragg. "That," she said, "is everything I know. I've told you frankly the entire situation."

Tragg, still regarding the onions in the sink, said, "I'm

glad you did. It always pays to be absolutely frank with the police."

She was talking quickly now, apparently giving him her fullest confidence. "It was," she explained, "Mr. Mason's idea that you shouldn't find him here. I, of course, didn't have any idea *why* you were coming. I'm terribly shocked to hear about Fred, but after all, I felt that I should tell you just exactly . . ."

Mason said, "Here's where I came in."

Tragg regarded him thoughtfully. "You mean here's where you go out."

In the doorway, Mason turned and smiled. "It amounts to the same thing as far as I'm concerned, Lieutenant."

4

■

There was a phone in the corner drugstore. Mason dropped a nickel and dialed his office, using the private unlisted number which rang the telephone on his own desk.

After several seconds, Della Street answered.

"Hello," Mason said cheerfully. "Had lunch?"

"Certainly not. You told me to wait right here."

"*I've* been to lunch."

"Well, I like that!"

"And we have a murder."

"Another one?"

"That's right."

"Who's the victim?"

"Fred Milfield."

"Chief!" she exclaimed. "How did it happen?"

"I don't know."

"Who's our client?"

Mason laughed. "We haven't one. Don't become such a slave to the conventions, Della. Can't I have a murder case without a client?"

"Not profitably."

"No," Mason admitted, "I suppose you have something there. Tell Paul Drake to get on the job, contact the newspaper boys, see what he can find out about Milfield's murder."

"Chief," she protested, "I've got to have someone to

27

charge this to—just as a matter of bookkeeping, and . . ."

"Okay," Mason said, "charge it to Miss Kingman."

"What," Della asked, "do you want Drake to find out about the murder?"

"Everything. You go get some eats. I'll be right up."

Mason flagged a taxi, went to his office and found Della Street waiting for him.

"Hello," Mason said, surprised, "I thought you'd gone to lunch."

"I was just starting out when I saw a well-dressed young woman frantically trying to get into the office, so I took pity on her and explained to her you wouldn't be in until Monday morning. She was white-faced and desperate, said she simply must see you."

Mason said impatiently, "I haven't time to see anyone now, Della. This murder case has broken. Milfield's been murdered. His wife was . . ."

"This young woman," Della Street interrupted, "is Carol Burbank."

"I don't care who she is. I . . . Oh! Wait a minute! Burbank, eh?"

Della Street nodded.

"Any relation to the Karakul fur Burbank?"

"I didn't know. That's why I let her in. I think she is."

Mason whistled. "We'll talk with Carol Burbank," he agreed. "She seems excited?"

"More than excited. She's white-faced with desperation."

"She's in the outer office?"

Della Street nodded.

Mason said, "Okay. You go down to Paul Drake's office. Tell him about Milfield's murder. Tell him the police know about it. He can dig out the details for us. Tell him to get busy on it and let everything else go. You talk with him and while you're doing that I'll see if this Carol Burbank is tied up with the Burbank we're looking for."

Della Street paused with her hand on the door. "How did Mrs. Milfield take it?" she asked.

Mason said, "I heard her scream. I don't think it was unexpected. She'd been crying when I got there."

"Attractive?"

"Very."

"Clever?"

"She threw me to the wolves."

Della Street raised her eyebrows.

"I was the sacrifice that enabled her to get in solid with Lieutenant Tragg."

"How come?" Della asked him.

Mason said, "Tragg called. I thought it would be better for her if he didn't find me there. She had been crying, you know, and Tragg's visit indicated a murder was in the wind. I ducked into the pantry. She told Tragg I was there."

"Why?"

"Apparently just to curry favor with him."

"How old?" Della Street asked.

"Somewhere around thirty."

"Sounds as though she could be dangerous," Della commented.

"I think she is."

"Okay, I'll get Paul Drake working on the Milfield case. Carol Burbank's waiting in the outer office."

Della Street ran down the long corridor, her feet echoing against the Saturday-afternoon silence of the business building. Mason went through the law library and into the reception office.

Carol Burbank was sitting very rigid, her knees pressed tightly together, her face a hard white mask, her mouth a garish red streak against make-up which refused to blend with the pale skin.

The convulsive start which shook her as the door latch clicked showed the state of her nerves. Big eyes turned to Mason.

There was no panic in those eyes, perhaps a trace of fear, but a resolute determination. She was a young woman who was trying desperately to keep control of herself and to keep her mind clear.

"Mr. Mason?"

"Yes."

"I believe you handled an automobile accident case yesterday—a Mr. Bickler who collided with a truck of the Skinner Hills Karakul Company?"

"That's right."

"My father thought you handled it very adroitly."

"Thank you."

"He mentioned that in case *we* ever had any trouble, it would be a good idea to get you on our side instead of having you on the other side."

"Your father is connected with the Karakul Sheep Company?" Mason asked.

"Indirectly."

"His name?"

"Roger Burbank."

"And I take it there's now been some trouble?"

She said, "Mr. Milfield, an associate of my father's, has been murdered—aboard my father's yacht."

"Indeed. What did you want me to do?"

"My father is in a very peculiar—a very precarious position. I want you to help him."

"He was aboard the yacht at the time the murder was committed?"

"Heavens no! That's the trouble. He wanted people to *think* he was aboard the yacht, but actually he wasn't there at *all*."

"Where is he?"

"I'm not certain that I know."

Mason said cautiously, "Before you say anything, Miss Burbank, I'd better tell you I'm afraid I can't represent your father."

"Why not?"

"I have an adverse interest."

"In what way?"

"Adelaide Kingman is the record owner of eighty acres that . . ."

"Frank Palermo really owns that property," she interrupted.

"I'm sorry, you're wrong."

"He's in possession."

"Under a contract of sale."

"But the contract isn't any good. He's been in possession for more than five years."

"Under that contract."

She hesitated a moment. "How much do you want?" she asked.

"Plenty."

"As sheep property, Mr. Mason, that's . . ."

"Virtually valueless," Mason interrupted. "As oil property it's valuable."

"Who said anything about oil?"

"I did."

Her eyes were searching and steady. "I'm afraid I don't get the connection."

"Adelaide Kingman," Mason said, "wants one hundred thousand dollars for that property in cash."

"That's absolutely absurd, Mr. Mason, that's outrageous."

"And that," Mason finished, "is why I'm afraid I can't represent your father."

She bit her lip. "That price is absolutely out of all reason, Mr. Mason."

Mason said cheerfully, "I'm sorry. Now you wanted an attorney to represent you, and it's Saturday afternoon, and I'm afraid you'll have some trouble finding . . ."

"We want you, Mr. Mason."

"I'm afraid I couldn't ethically represent you as long as I have an adverse . . ."

"Look here," she said, "we'll let that ride. If you'll

31

represent Father you can continue to handle the Kingman property and when you meet Father, drive the best bargain you can."

"It's going to be a hard bargain," Mason warned.

"I expect that—now."

"You have the right to speak for your father?"

"Yes, in an emergency of this kind, I do. I know I do."

Mason said, "I wouldn't want to have any misunderstanding about that."

"There won't be."

"And what do you want me to do?"

"I want you to go to my father with me. We've simply got to find him."

"What's he doing?"

"He's working on something so vitally important that it's absolutely essential he has complete secrecy. No one would have been permitted to know where he was or what he was doing.—Don't you see the position in which that leaves him?"

"On account of the murder?"

"Yes. Fred Milfield was murdered on his yacht. Dad usually goes out every Friday night on his yacht and anchors in the estuary. It's his method of letting down, of getting away from business. This Friday he took the yacht out and anchored it as usual, but he didn't stay there. He's working on a thing that's so big and so important that— well, he'd never admit to *anyone* what he was doing."

"Do you know where he is?"

"I have a general idea. I hope I can find him. And we've got to get there before the police do. We simply *have* to get there before the police do, Mr. Mason, Do you understand?"

"Why?"

"So we can tell him what's happened."

"The police will tell him."

"They'll trap him into certain declarations first."

"Such as what?"

"Don't you see, Mr. Mason? Father's working on something that's so vitally important he would walk right into a trap in the event the police started questioning him."

"You mean he'd swear he was aboard the yacht at the time it will turn out the murder was committed?"

"Yes."

"And if we get to him in time?" Mason asked.

"Then we could explain things to him."

"And then what?"

"Then he'd have a chance to think up what he really wanted to tell the police."

"Some good lie?"

"Of course not. He'd tell them as much of the truth as he dared."

"I think I'll have to know a little more than that. What's he doing?"

"It has something to do with a political situation. I think they're gunning for some of the political big-shots in the oil industry, and Dad was getting some of the groundwork done. It would be absolutely suicidal to let that stuff get out before all the plans have been made in detail."

"I see."

"So we've got to find him."

Mason's fingertips drummed on the desk. "You have a lot more to work on than I have. Just what is my status, anyway?"

"I want to retain you."

"For what?"

"To protect my father's interests."

"Anyone else?"

"Well—you might say to act as a family attorney—sort of a general assignment."

"Just what are we going to do?"

"We'll go places."

"Where?"

"That's so confidential I won't even tell *you* in advance. You take your hat and your overcoat, and we walk out of the office, starting now." Once more she glanced swiftly at her watch.

"When do I get back?"

"After we've found Father."

Mason led the way back to his private office, opened the door of the hat closet, took his overcoat and hat, turned to Carol Burbank, "Are you ready?"

For the third time, she looked at her watch, started to say something, then changed her mind, said instead, "Yes. All ready."

As they passed the door of the Drake Detective Agency, Mason opened the door, called, "Della!"

Della Street emerged from one of the inner offices.

Mason closed his left eye. "I'm going out," he said. "You go get some eats. Don't wait for me."

"When will you be back, Chief?"

It was Carol Burbank who answered the question. "It's indefinite," she said quite firmly.

5

Carol Burbank tucked her hand under Mason's arm, said, "This way," and led him from the exit of the building down the street for half a block and into a parking space.

"He should be here," she said, looking around at the people nearby, and frowning.

"Who—your father?"

"No. Judson Beltin."

"Who's Judson Beltin?"

"My father's right-hand man."

"He knows about the murder?"

"Yes."

"He knows where you're going?"

"No."

After a few moments she reconsidered her curt answer and said, "Judson doesn't know anything except that he's to get the car and fill it absolutely chock-full of gasoline, and have a couple of five-gallon cans in the trunk. He was to be here five minutes ago and wait for me. Of course, I realize he may have some trouble, but . . . Here he comes now."

A car, being driven rapidly through traffic, slid in front of another car, and, in one continuous gliding motion, turned into the parking lot.

"That's Beltin. Don't let on he means anything to us,"

35

Carol warned. "Just stand here as though we were waiting for a car to be delivered to us."

"Why all the mystery?"

"Please," she pleaded, "trust me. I can't explain. Just wait and do what I tell you to."

A slender man of around thirty-five with a distinctive stoop turned the car over to an attendant who collected twenty-five cents, tore off a perforated numbered slip of pasteboard and handed it to him. Leaving the parking station, Beltin walked directly past Carol Burbank and Mason. He gave no sign of recognition, but his hand flashed out, and Carol's hand closed on the oblong of pasteboard.

Carol said, "Let's see if someone follows him. . . . There—there's the man! See. He got out of that parked automobile. See—he's following Judson."

Mason said, "After all, this is a busy city street. If you'll turn around in this locality at any given instant and look behind you, you'll find a couple of hundred people streaming along behind. Does that mean they're following you?"

She didn't say anything, but waited until Judson had turned the corner. Then she was careful to pick a service station attendant other than the one who had parked Beltin's car. Quite calmly she handed him the parking ticket, and waited until the car had been brought out to the parking station exit. Then she slid in behind the steering wheel, waited while Mason got in beside her, then sent the car purring forward, pausing for a stop in front of the curb, then adroitly manipulating it out into traffic, driving with a smooth competence which elicited Mason's enthusiastic although silent approval.

"Now," she said, "just to make certain that we aren't being followed."

She swung the car abruptly to the left, just in front of an oncoming horde of traffic that had started forward in a rush at the change of the traffic signal.

"Anyone coming?" she asked as she straightened out.

Mason took a long breath, didn't even look around. "If anyone had been following us, we'd have heard the smash by this time."

She turned to the right at the next corner, slowed until she ran into another closed signal. Then, at the change of light, sent the car leaping forward once more to cut across the line of oncoming traffic, just as she had done at the other crossing.

Having convinced herself that no one was following her, she settled down behind the wheel to the job of driving, taking the car out through Hollywood, over the Cahuenga Grade, out Ventura Boulevard, constantly crowding speed from the car, getting it well out in front whenever she came to slower moving vehicles going in the same direction. Mason respected her silence by settling back in the cushions and smoking cigarettes.

They topped the slight incline above the Conejo Grade, then went rushing down the mountains and into Camarillo. She was once more watching her wrist watch as she drove into Ventura.

"I hope," she said, "we'll be in time."

Those were the first words she had uttered since leaving Los Angeles.

Mason said nothing.

Midway between Ventura and Santa Barbara she suddenly slowed, then pulled into a "Motel" where neat stucco bungalows and red tiled roofs contrasted against green palm fronds and the dark blue of the ocean in the background.

"Do we get out?" Mason asked.

"Yes."

Mason followed her into the office of the manager.

"You have a Mr. J. C. Lassing registered here?" she asked.

The manager looked at her register. "Cottage fourteen. There's a party of five."

37

"Thank you," Carol said, giving the woman her brightest smile, and nodding to Mason.

They walked down a crunching gravel driveway. The sun, dipping low in the west, was casting elongated shadows along the buildings, and, now that they were out of the car, they became conscious of a cold wind lashing the channel into whitecaps, a wind which forced Carol to lean forward, pressing her skirt down against her knees.

The cabin they wanted seemed dark and silent. There was no car in the garage.

Carol ran up the three cement steps and pounded frantically against the door. When there was no answer, she tried the knob.

The door was unlocked, and the wind behind them blew the door open as the knob was turned.

Carol Burbank jumped forward, caught at the door just as it slammed against a rubber door stop. "I guess," she said with a nervous laugh, "we go on in."

Mason entered behind her, shouldered the door closed. He raised his voice and called, "Hello—is anyone home?"

There was no answer.

The cabin was a large four-room building which could be shut off into two double cottages. The big room in the front had twin beds and was spacious enough to serve as a commodious sitting room as well. The furniture was comparable to that of a high-class hotel. The beds were all neatly made. Around the davenport, three chairs had been grouped in a semicircle, and it seemed that every ashtray in the house had been pressed into service. There was a litter of cigarette stubs and cigar butts. On a taboret reposed five glasses. And the wastebasket beside the davenport was filled with empty bottles both of liquor and of mixers. About the room was the stench of cold cigar butts, and the odor of stale liquor.

Carol said, "I'm afraid they've left. Let's take a look through the place and see if there's any baggage."

She led the way through the various rooms.

There was no sign of baggage. The bathrooms contained soiled towels. On one of the bathroom shelves was a safety razor and a shaving brush. Carol looked at it, picked up the brush and exclaimed, "It's Father's!"

"Perhaps he's coming back," Mason said.

"No, his bag's gone. He just left the shaving things here. He's forgetful about things like that."

"You don't think he'll be back?"

"No. This cabin has served the purpose for which it was rented."

"What was that?"

"A political conference. Some of the bigwigs from Sacramento. I can't tell you who they were, and I wouldn't dare to hint even to you what they were talking about. It's political dynamite, something so big, something so stupendous that a premature disclosure would ruin the political careers of the men who took part in the conference."

"All right," Mason told her. "This is your party. What do you want to do next?"

She said, "Nothing. I'll just pick up Father's shaving things and take them along. There's nothing else we can do."

Mason said nothing.

Carol hesitated, then slowly picked up the shaving brush and contemplated the safety razor on the glass shelf.

"He didn't even clean it," she said. And then to Mason, "Do you think I should wash it off and clean it?"

"That all depends."

"On what?"

"On whether you think it's important to establish the fact that your father was here."

"He wouldn't ever admit that he was here."

"Why not?"

"I've explained to you. It would be political suicide for the people who were here . . ."

"It wouldn't hurt your *father's* career any, would it?"

"What wouldn't?"

"If it were known that he was here."

"No, not my father. I'm thinking of the others."

"Suppose your father didn't mention their names?"

"Why? What good would that do?"

"Just in case," Mason said, "your father needs to show where he was yesterday night, that razor might be a bit of corroborative evidence. Microscopic examination of hairs, you know."

Her face lit up with sudden realization of the import of Mason's words. "You're right!" she exclaimed. "How right you are!"

"You could," Mason observed, "stop by the manager's office, explain to her that you wish to keep this same cabin for a week, pay the rent on it in cash, and stipulate that it be left absolutely as it is, that no one be permitted to enter the cabin, not even the chambermaids."

"That's an idea!" she exclaimed. "Come on!"

Mason said, "We should be able to lock that front door. You don't see a key around anywhere, do you?"

They searched the place and could find no key. The door from the cabin number thirteen was locked and the key was on the inside, but there was no key for the door to cabin fourteen.

"That seems to be it," Mason said. "Where do you suppose your father is now?"

Her eyes showed panic at his question. "He's gone back to the yacht," she said in dismay. "The police will be waiting to question him, and he'll tell them some awful fib about where he was—anything to keep from admitting that he was here."

Mason said, "Let's go make our arrangements with the front office, then get back to Los Angeles, and try to find your father."

Mason held the door open for Carol, watched appreciatively as the wind whipped her skirt high on her shapely legs. Then she fought the skirt down and Mason pulled the door shut against the cold west wind blowing in from the ocean.

"You do the talking to the manager," she said. And then suddenly added, "Here, you'd better have some money for expenses."

She pushed a sheaf of bills into his hand. Mason looked down at it. They were twenty-dollar bills and were fastened together with a gummed paper which bore the imprint of a Los Angeles bank, and the amount of money contained in the sheaf of bills—five hundred dollars.

Mason said, "It'll hardly be this much."

"Keep it. You'll have other expenses. Just keep an account of them and we'll adjust later."

Mason slipped the bills into the side pocket of his coat, entered the cabin marked OFFICE and stood waiting at the counter until the woman who acted as manager came out.

Her smile was an automatic reflex.

"Find the people you want?" she asked.

Mason assumed his most magnetic manner. "The situation," he explained, "is rather peculiar, and somewhat complicated."

The smile immediately faded from the woman's face. Her eyes were cold and hard as she shifted them from Mason to a glittering appraisal of the young girl at his side.

"Yes?" she asked coldly. "In what way is the situation complicated, please?"

Mason said, "We were looking for this young woman's father. He was to have met us in cabin fourteen, but we were late and I'm afraid he's gone on to try and pick us up on the road. We'll have to go and get in touch with him."

The woman's expression remained one of hard, cold appraisal. She said nothing, but waited as Mason paused, giving him no sign of encouragement.

41

"So," Mason went on, "I think the only thing for us to do is to see that you don't rent this cabin again."

"Rent is paid until tomorrow at twelve o'clock," she said.

"Does the registration show the names of all the parties who occupied the cabin?" Mason asked.

"Why?"

"I want to be absolutely certain that this is the party we want."

"Was the name Lassing?"

Carol said hastily, "That's the name of one of the members of the party, but not my father's name. I'm wondering if they were all registered."

"What's your father's name, dearie?" the woman asked.

Carol Burbank met her eyes steadily. "Burbank," she said. "Roger Burbank."

The woman softened somewhat. "We don't usually keep registrations of all the members of the party—where it's a large party. One man registers, usually the owner of the automobile, but he writes the make and license number of the car. Just a minute and I'll look it up."

She turned to a book of records and said, "No, the registration is just *J. C. Lassing and party*."

Mason said, "The cabin is all made up. There's no necessity for anyone going in there until tomorrow morning."

"Why *should* anyone go in there?" the manager asked.

"The chambermaids," Mason said, "might be changing towels."

"Well, what of it?"

"We'd prefer to have the cabin left exactly the way it is."

"The rent," the woman said coldly, "is eight dollars a day."

Mason handed her forty dollars. "That will pay the rent for five days."

She seemed somewhat mollified as she looked at the money. "You want a receipt?" she asked.

Mason's voice was as cold as hers had been.

"Certainly."

parted suddenly. She said...
looking reflexive, thanks the va...
he was... left gone more now...

6

■

"Any ideas?" Carol asked Mason as they drove out of the motel and she turned the car back toward Los Angeles.

"It's still your party," Mason said, and then asked after a moment, "Do you plan to have refreshments?"

She smiled. "Hungry?"

"Practically starved. That cold wind gives me an appetite."

"We'll eat down the road a ways. I want very much to find Father."

"Don't you think it's too late for that? Don't you think the police have rounded him up by this time?"

"Probably."

The sun had dipped below the horizon, leaving the ocean a steely blue, the surface lashed into restless turmoil by the wind. Over to the right, the Channel Islands were silhouetted sharply against the greenish blue of the western sky.

"Guess we'd better have lights," Carol said, and switched on the headlights.

It was after they had passed Ventura and were approaching Camarillo that Mason said, "How long ago do you suppose your father actually left that motel?"

She took her eyes from the road long enough to flash him a quick glance. "I don't know. Why?"

"I was just wondering."

"I have no means of knowing."

44

"I see."

The car purred smoothly up the Conejo Grade, ran past a rolling plateau country that was studded with huge live oaks. The wind had gone down now and the stars of early evening were resplendent in a sky that was clear as crystal. Far out in the country, they encountered the sign indicating the city limits of Los Angeles, and fifteen or twenty minutes later, Carol Burbank said abruptly, "There's a restaurant ahead where my father usually eats when he's on the road. There's just a chance we might find him there—if he didn't leave that motor lodge until sometime late in the afternoon."

"In which event," Mason said, "we must have passed him on the road."

"I feel certain we must have done just that," she said. "It's that one ahead, the red sign that says 'DOBE HUT RESTAURANT.'"

Mason said nothing.

Carol, manipulating the car into a parking place, switched off the ignition and threw up the catch on the left-hand door. It was as she was fitting the key to the lock on the door, that Mason indicated the red spotlight on a car parked in the opposite row. "Looks like the police eat here too," he said.

"Oh yes, the highway patrols eat here, and . . ."

"That's not a highway patrol car."

Carol said nothing, so Mason, clasping her forearm lightly with his fingers, guided her through the doorway of the 'dobe house.

The dining room held some fifteen tables. On the side opposite the door was a huge fireplace, and in this fireplace crackling oak logs furnished a cheery warmth. A hostess, dressed in a Spanish dancing costume, with very dark hair, intense black eyes, and lips heavy with make-up, flashed a smile at Mason, piloted the way toward a table.

Suddenly, Carol gave a half exclamation, veered toward

45

the left-hand corner, and approached a table where three men were talking.

Mason saw a powerfully built man with a closely cropped gray mustache and keen gray eyes glance up at her, saw the smile on his face, heard Carol say, "Hello, Dad! What on earth are *you* doing here?"

The three men got to their feet. Mason, coming over behind Carol, bowed to the man with the gray mustache and said, "Mr. Roger Burbank, I presume."

"Perry Mason, Father. You know, he's the lawyer," Carol explained hastily.

Burbank's thick-fingered, powerful hand shot across the table, gripped the lawyer's hand.

"And Lieutenant Tragg," Mason said, smiling into Tragg's somewhat puzzled countenance. "Permit me to introduce Carol Burbank, Lieutenant. And I take it the gentleman with you is from the Homicide Squad?"

"George Avon," Tragg admitted. And then after a moment, as though debating whether to disclose the information, added, "fingerprint expert."

Mason shook hands with Avon.

"Won't you be seated?" Roger Burbank asked politely.

The hostess, flashing white teeth in a smile, came over to the table. "I didn't know that you were joining friends," she said. "Waiter, two chairs at once, please."

The waiter brought two chairs and Mason held the chair for Carol Burbank, then seated himself. "We were famished," he announced.

Tragg said dryly, "It didn't take your reinforcements long to get here, did it, Burbank?"

Burbank raised his eyebrows. "My reinforcements?"

"Your attorney."

Burbank said, "I'm afraid there's some mistake. *I* didn't send for Mr. Mason."

"Haven't you told him yet?" Carol demanded of Tragg.

Tragg said, "I haven't been here long. I've been asking a few questions."

"Told me what?" Burbank demanded of Carol.

Tragg interrupted. "I want to get this straight, Mr. Burbank. It has become important to know exactly where you were and what you were doing yesterday afternoon and evening. So far you've done a lot of stalling. Now suppose you start talking."

"Why should my whereabouts mean anything to you?" Mason said, "Come, come, gentlemen. Let's be fair."

Carol Burbank said, "Dad, you've *got* to tell these men *exactly* where you were. You don't need to tell them the names of the other persons who were with you if you don't want to. But you've got to tell them where you were and when you went there. It's important."

Mason said suavely, "Fred Milfield was murdered aboard your yacht."

Lieutenant Tragg made a gesture of irritation. "That's what comes of trying to be polite! I should have taken you to Headquarters the minute I walked in, and questioned you there."

"*Fred Milfield murdered!*" Burbank exclaimed.

"That's right, Dad. We've been trying to find you all afternoon."

"And you thought it necessary to bring a lawyer along with you?" Tragg asked.

Carol faced him with cold steady eyes. "Certainly. And if you knew all the facts of the case . . ."

Burbank said, "I simply can't understand why anyone would want to murder Fred Milfield. You're sure he was murdered, Lieutenant?"

Carol said, "Dad, won't you trust my judgment? Please, *please,* won't you tell them?"

Roger Burbank said, "Let's hear what Lieutenant Tragg has to say first."

Carol said to Lieutenant Tragg impatiently, "Dad *wasn't* there at all yesterday afternoon. Father has been mixing into politics—there are things that have to be kept absolutely confidential. Even now, I can't tell you the details—

47

but suppose Dad had an appointment with some big-shots from Sacramento—people who insisted that their meeting be shrouded with the utmost secrecy. He simply couldn't tell you who they were, and each of them would deny it if you put the question up to him. Suppose they took every precaution to insure secrecy, and met at a motor lodge up here on the coast highway, were in conference for nearly twenty-four hours, working out plans, and only split up a short time ago. I thought he might stop in here for dinner. I took a chance on stopping—and here we are."

"How very, very interesting," Tragg said. "You say that none of these men would admit he was present at the conference?"

"None of them would dare to."

Tragg said, "All right. Let's quit beating around the bush. If there's anything to this, we want to know it, and check on it—and if there isn't," and here Tragg's voice became ominously crisp, "we want to find that out too."

"You tell them, Dad," Carol said.

Burbank said nothing. His forehead was creased in a dark scowl of disapproval as he frowned at his daughter.

"All right," Carol said, "if I have to, I will. You investigate at the Surf and Sun Motel up on the highway between Ventura and Santa Barbara. The big place over on the left out on . . ."

"Yes, I know where it is," Tragg said. "And that's where this conference was held?"

"Just go there."

Tragg turned to Burbank. "If there's anything to this, you'd better verify it."

Burbank seemed angry. "Oh well," he said with a gesture of annoyance, "she's let the cat out of the bag now. But *I'm* not going to confirm it. If you ask me I'll—damn it, I'll deny it."

"Any proof?" Tragg asked Carol.

"Of course there's proof—if you get right at it. The ashtrays and empty bottles are still there. Get fingerprints.

We told the manager to leave things just as they were. Dad even left his shaving outfit on the glass shelf in the bathroom."

"By George!" Burbank exclaimed, "I'm always forgetting that damned razor."

Tragg said dryly, "Any real evidence except that of the shaving kit?"

Carol said, "Dad, didn't you carry the key away with you? It isn't at the motel."

Slowly Roger Burbank slipped his hand into the side pocket of his coat, pulled out a typical hotel key, from the loop of which dangled a chain. Attached to the chain was a large papier-mâché tag imprinted SURF AND SUN MOTEL, and down below in large numerals the figure *14*.

On the other side was the usual stamped notice stating that if the key was inadvertently carried away, it was necessary only to place a postage stamp on it and drop it in any mailbox.

Tragg took the key, scraped back his chair, signaled the waiter. "Cancel our orders," he said, "and give the check to the wise guy."

He jabbed an angry finger in Mason's direction.

7

A light was on in Mason's office as the lawyer's rubber heels padded down the tiled floor of the corridor. He quietly fitted a latchkey to the door, clicked back the lock, and pushed the door open.

Della Street was seated at Mason's desk, her head pillowed on her arm. She was fast asleep.

Mason gently closed the door, hung up his hat and coat, walked across to the desk and stood for a moment looking down at Della with tender solicitude. Then he slid his hand along her hair, let it rest on the back of her shoulders.

"Don't you ever go home?" he asked tenderly.

Della wakened with a start, turned her head, blinked her eyes against the light and smiled up at Mason. "I had to know what happened," she said. "That meant I had to wait."

"Bosh! You were waiting because you thought I might ring up and want something. Had any dinner?"

"No."

"Lunch?"

"I had Gertie go out and bring in a couple of sandwiches and a bottle of milk."

Mason said, "I'm going to keep you with me after this —at least you'll eat regularly."

"What's new?" she asked.

Mason studied her face intently, saw traces of fatigue.

50

"The thing that's new," he said, "is that you're going home and get yourself some shuteye."

"What time is it?"

"Something after eleven."

"Heavens! I've been asleep for over an hour."

"Where's Paul Drake?"

"He went home."

"That's where you're going. Come on, get your things."

"I was afraid you might call," she said. "I . . ."

"Forget it," Mason interrupted. "I have the number of your apartment. I could have called you there. Don't take this job so seriously."

"What happened?" she asked.

"We had a very nice ride up the coast," Mason told her, helping her into her coat. "We went up to a very nice motel. We really must stop in there sometime, Della. It has a beautiful location. It's called the Surf and Sun, and, while today there was a cold, raw wind blowing in from the ocean, I can imagine that it would be very delightful, particularly during the summer."

"Did you find Roger Burbank?"

"Yes. But not up there."

"Where was he?"

"In a restaurant about half an hour away from here on the Ventura Boulevard—an old adobe house taken over and turned into a restaurant."

"What does the motel have to do with it?"

"Well," Mason said, "it seems that Burbank is supposed to have met some big-shot politicians up there—people who exerted every precaution to see that their motions couldn't be traced. Burbank, for instance, was supposed to have been aboard his yacht. Apparently every one of these men had laid careful plans so he could deny having attended any such conference."

"Why?"

"The men were big-shots. Perhaps the governor himself was there. They were planning some political strategy.

51

If the newspapers had got hold of it, it would have been dynamite."

"Was the governor really there?"

Mason said, "Well, the significant fact may have been that *he* wasn't invited."

"You mean some of the legislative leaders were plotting against him?"

"Yes, it could have been that—the way Carol told it."

Della frowned. "I can see where it would be very inconvenient to have a murder committed on one's yacht under these circumstances."

Mason said, "And then again . . ." He broke off to push his tongue against his cheek so that it made a big lump.

"What's that," Della asked, "chewing tobacco?"

"No. Just to show you that I have my tongue in my cheek. Come on, young lady. Switch out the lights."

She switched out the lights. Mason waited for the door to click shut, then tried the knob to make certain it was locked.

As they started down the corridor, he said, "It seems that Lieutenant Tragg and a fingerprint man by the name of Avon had located Burbank at this restaurant shortly before we got there—just a minute or two, I guess."

"This was at that adobe restaurant?"

"Yes."

"And what happened?"

"Carol told her father he simply must tell where he'd been, and finally the old man quit denying he'd been there."

"Rather a peculiar position for a man to be in, wasn't it?" Della asked. "I mean, telling the police that he'd been with several men who would have to deny that they had been there with him?"

"Very," Mason admitted. "It was a poser for Tragg. And the hell of it is, as far as Tragg's concerned, he's dealing with political big-shots. If he takes Burbank's word that he wasn't aboard that yacht when the murder was committed, that's one thing. If he insists upon corroboration and starts checking up, he may stir up a hornet's nest. Tragg, you see, is more or less dependent upon having a certain amount of political good-will."

Mason rang for the elevator.

"Was there any corroborating evidence whatever?"

"Very strong corroborating evidence," Mason said, "and produced at the psychological moment in a manner well calculated to carry conviction."

"Just what was it?"

"Burbank's hand dropped down to his coat pocket. He produced the key to the cottage that had been occupied by the politicians—a key that undoubtedly came from cabin fourteen at the Surf and Sun Motel."

"What did Tragg say to that?"

"That," Mason said, "convinced Tragg so much that he jumped up from the table and went whizzing up the highway. Lieutenant Tragg never lets eating interfere with business."

"You mean he passed up his dinner?"

"Didn't even wait for the food to be brought, and it was a swell dinner. Green turtle soup. Then nice sizzling steak, and salad, with a dish of chili beans on the side and tortillas. . . ."

"Chief! are you trying to make me hungry?"

"Are you hungry?"

"I hadn't realized it. Guess I was just—well, I guess I haven't gotten around to realize it, but I *am* hungry."

"That," Mason announced, "is as it should be. You're going to get something hot to eat—and I don't ever again want to hear of you sticking around that stuffy office Saturday afternoons and nights. What has Paul found out about the murder?"

"I have a written report here. It gives the highlights. Come to think of it, I haven't thought about the newspapers. It should make the late evening edition."

Mason again jabbed his thumb against the elevator button, held it there for several seconds. "You," he announced, "are going to have a cocktail, some hot soup and a steak."

"A little hot soup would taste good," she admitted. "Where do we go?"

"Down to that chummy little restaurant on Ninth Street. We can get a booth there and talk. Where's Drake's report?"

"In my purse."

"Okay. We'll stroll over and get a table."

The janitor brought up the elevator, gave Mason the benefit of a frowning rebuke for that long second ring.

Mason and Della rode down in silence, then out on the street, smiled at each other in silent comment on the janitor's grouch, walked up Ninth Street arm in arm, turned into a little unpretentious restaurant where they knew the proprietor, and found seats in a curtained booth near the entrance.

The proprietor, a huge florid figure of a lusty man, attired in a chef's cap and apron, came in to give them a welcome.

"Ah—ze great Perry MASON! And zat so charming Della Strit! Welcome! Pierre weeth hees own hands cooks you ze food an' serves you ze dreenks!"

"That's fine," Mason said. "We are honored. A dry Martini for Della, a Scotch and soda for me. Then a nice filet mignon for Della with some au gratin potatoes and coffee for two. Do you happen to have a nice filet mignon, Pierre?"

"For Miss Strit, yes! Anything she wants. Right away queek I get you these drinks."

He backed through the curtained doorway. Della opened her purse, handed Mason Paul Drake's report of what he had been able to find out about the murder. "There are some three-and-a-quarter by four-and-a-quarter photographs attached to it," she said. "Paul says he can get some blown-up enlargements by tomorrow or Monday."

The proprietor brought them their drinks, stood beaming over them with a certain paternal solicitude. "You come here and talk business! With so pretty a girl was Pierre twenty years younger—Poof! Business!"

Mason touched glasses across the table with Della Street, sipped his drink, then abruptly reached across the table to put his hand over hers. "Okay, Della, we're going to take it easy from now on. You've always said it would be a lot better if I sat in the office the way other lawyers do and let people come to me. Pierre is right. We talk too damn much business."

Della said demurely, "You'd better glance through Paul's report."

Mason started to say something and then changed his mind, unfolded Drake's report and glanced at it casually.

It was a neatly typewritten report, and the first page read:

SUMMARY

Perry: This is a recapitulation of the detailed information and photographs you will find on the following pages. Roger Burbank is a financier. Ordinarily he doesn't go in for speculative investments. Fred Milfield and Harry Van Nuys got Burbank to finance the Skinner Hills sheep project—whatever that may be. Probably your hunch on the oil is the right one. I don't think the police have stumbled onto Van Nuys yet. My men have now located him at the Cornish Hotel and are keeping an eye on him.

The murder was committed aboard Burbank's yacht sometimes early Friday evening. It's a sailing yacht about thirty-five feet in length, and Burbank uses it as a means of escape, not to cruise in. He usually goes out Friday nights, and at high tide goes in on the mud flats and amuses himself spearing sharks. When the tide begins to go out he anchors in the channel, reads books, studies, and loafs. Occasionally a chap named Beltin, who is his right-hand man, comes out to relay some message of importance. Once or twice Milfield has gone out to the yacht, apparently by prearrangement. Once he brought Van Nuys with him. Burbank is a crank about sails. There isn't even an auxiliary motor on the boat. An outboard motor for the dinghy with about five gallons of gasoline is as far as he'll go. Even the cooking and heating are done on a wood stove. Lighting is by candle. The body was found rolled over against the starboard side of the cabin, but there is evidence to indicate the murder took place on the port side of the cabin and when the boat went aground at low tide, the body rolled over. Death was caused by a single crushing blow on the back of the head, and so far I haven't been able to get too many details about the police theory. One outstanding clue is the print of a *woman's* shoe outlined in blood on the lower tread of the companionway right in the middle of the step. The police consider it a major clue. I've got the names, addresses, location of the yacht club, a sketch plan of the yacht, and the reports of my operatives attached hereto. This is just a summary. I'll be waiting for a call from you in case you want me. Della says she doesn't know when you'll be back.

PAUL.

Mason ran through the papers that were attached to Drake's report, studied the photographs. Della Street watched him silently, finishing her cocktail, smoking a cigarette.

Pierre brought food, frowned at Mason's abstraction, said gallantly to Della Street, "To be twenty years younger, I give my right arm. No," he amended abruptly, "weeth twenty years younger Pierre need hees right arm."

Mason looked up and grinned. "It's a good line, Pierre. Look, you've got a long extension on your desk telephone. Hand it over here, will you? I want to make a call."

Pierre sighed. "Always business," he remonstrated. "So it was when I was young, too—but a different kind, you bet!"

He left the booth, handed a desk telephone on a long extension cord across the top of the partition. Mason dialed Paul Drake's number and held his lips close to the telephone so that his voice would be inaudible beyond the confines of the booth.

When Drake came on the line Mason said, "Hello, Paul. Got a pencil handy?"

"Yes."

"Okay, make a note of this. J. C. Lassing, L-a-s-s-i-n-g. Got that, Paul?"

"Uh huh."

"Okay," Mason said. "Now make a note of the Surf and Sun Motel on the highway between Ventura and Santa Barbara, got that?"

"Uh huh."

"All right. J. C. Lassing is supposed to have registered at cabin fourteen at the Surf and Sun Motel yesterday. I'd like to know a lot more about Mr. Lassing."

"All right, I'll get busy."

"I'm just reading your report," Mason said. "Who discovered the body, Paul?"

"A sheep man by the name of Palermo. Wanted to see Milfield and knew he was aboard Burbank's yacht."

"How'd he get aboard?" Mason asked.

"Palermo's a tight-fisted son of the soil," Drake answered. "He was damned if he was going to pay fifty cents to rent a rowboat when he had a folding boat he could use. There's a lake up in that Skinner Hills district where they do a lot of duck shooting and Palermo guides dudes around at ten bucks a day, furnishing boat and decoys. So

57

he loaded his folding boat into a trailer and carried it along."

"Just to save fifty cents?" Mason asked.

"That's his story. I haven't talked with him. The newspaper boys say it sounds convincing once you've seen the guy. Here's something else, Perry. Van Nuys told the clerk at the hotel where he's staying that if he hadn't stopped Mrs. Milfield from taking a plane to San Francisco yesterday afternoon, she'd have been in a sweet mess by this time. My man was hanging around the lobby and managed to overhear enough of the conversation to get the general drift."

"Nice going, Paul. I'll see what he has to say about it."

"Keep my man out of it if you can."

"Okay," Mason said. "You get in touch with Lassing. I think I'll have a talk with Van Nuys right away—if I can beat the police to it. He's at the Cornish Hotel?"

"According to the last report I had he is," Drake said.

"When was that report?"

"About thirty minutes ago."

"Okay," Mason said. "I'll look him up. How does it happen the police have overlooked him?"

"The police apparently don't know too much about the Skinner Hills business. Remember we started working on that Karakul fur deal and that's given us the inside track."

"Okay," Mason said, "I'll call you if anything turns up."

"I'll be getting reports until around two or two-thirty," Drake said, "but for the love of Mike, don't call me after that unless it's something damned important."

Mason hung up, pushed the telephone to one side. "How's the grub, Della?"

"Fine. Tell me about Carol."

"What about her?"

"Why did you have your tongue in your cheek when you came back?"

58

Mason reached into the side pocket of his coat, took out the sheaf of twenty-dollar bills Carol had given him.

"What's that?" Della asked him.

"Expense money."

"It looks as though she thought you were going to have plenty of expenses."

"Doesn't it?"

"What's the idea?"

Mason said, "When do the banks close, Della?"

"What do you mean? Oh, I see. It's Saturday."

"Exactly. Here we have five hundred dollars in twenty-dollar bills. They are fastened together with a gummed strip of paper bearing the imprint of the Seaboard National Trust and Savings Bank. Nice new bills—interesting, isn't it?"

"You mean Carol drew this expense money out of the bank before . . ."

"Exactly."

"But she didn't know about the murder before noon, did she?"

Mason grinned. "I didn't ask her. I was careful not to. What would you do, Della, if you found yourself faced with the job of manufacturing an alibi?"

"You mean, if I had to make an alibi up out of whole cloth?"

"Yes."

"Heavens! I don't know. It would seem to me to be an impossible problem."

Mason said, "Even if you had a long, long time to think it over, I'll bet you couldn't do a better job than to claim that you'd been attending a political conference of such great importance the bigwigs who attended it wouldn't dare to let their identities be known, would even deny that they were there. And then if you could lead some witness into a place where that conference took place and point to ash trays that were littered with cigar butts and cigarette stubs, a wastebasket that was filled with empty bottles, bathrooms containing soiled towels, and, even as a final finishing touch, 'Father's razor on the shelf in the bathroom'—that, I would say, would be a very artistic job."

"Very."

"Then if the police happened to discover 'Father' at just the opportune moment, and 'Father' seemed not at all eager to establish his alibi, but only did so under pressure, and then rather reluctantly put his hand down into his coat pocket and pulled out a key to the cabin in which the conference was supposed to have taken place—that would be one sweet job of alibi building, wouldn't it?"

"Do you think the whole thing was faked?"

"I don't know. I'm just pointing out things."

"But can't the police check every detail?"

"Which do you mean, *can* or will?"

"What's the difference?"

"Query: What would *you* do if you were a police officer —and had to decide whether you wanted to rip aside the mask of secrecy some big-shot politicians had carefully set up?"

Della said, "Well, I *might* try to dig out the truth, and then again, I might drop the whole thing—fast."

"Exactly," Mason said.

"Apparently," Della Street said thoughtfully, "Carol Burbank is a very unusual girl."

"Or her father is a very unusual man," Mason said. "I'm interested in finding out which—and in the meantime, finish your dinner because you're going home and get some sleep."

Della Street smiled across the table at him. "Not if you're going to beat the police to the Hotel Cornish. A notebook might come in handy there."

Mason smiled. "It's going to cost you your dessert."

"I didn't want any, anyway."

"That'll run Pierre's blood pressure up."

Della Street opened her purse, calmly started applying

lipstick. "One gathers," she said, "that Pierre's blood pressure has been boiling up and dropping down at alternate intervals for the last forty years."

"That," Mason said, "would have made it start when Pierre was about fourteen."

"Well," Della Street announced, putting her lipstick and compact back into her purse, "let's make it forty-*two* years then."

8

The Hotel Cornish was one of the less pretentious hotels tucked away on the fringes of the business district. The night clerk, a man somewhere in the late sixties, with a high forehead, fuzzy hair that bristled out on each side above the ears, looked at Perry Mason and Della Street through rimless glasses and said shortly, "Full up. There isn't a room in the house."

Mason said, "You have a Harry Van Nuys registered here?"

"That's right. Van Nuys, Las Vegas, Nevada, room 618. Want to leave a message?"

"I'd like to have you call him and let him know I'm here."

"He expecting you?"

"Not exactly."

"It's late."

"I know what time it is."

The clerk hesitated, then with somewhat poor grace plugged in a line and said, "A lady and a gentleman down here to see you."

He waited a moment then turned his head over his shoulder.

"What's that name again?" he asked.

"Mason."

The clerk said into the telephone, "It's a Mr. Mason. . . . Very well. I wasn't certain whether you had retired."

The clerk pulled out the plug, said somewhat ungraciously, "You can go up."

Mason nodded to Della Street.

It was an automatic elevator and it seemed to take an interminable time rattling and swaying up to the sixth floor.

Harry Van Nuys was waiting for them at the door of 618.

Mason had an opportunity to size up the man as slender fingers clasped about Mason's. "Mr. Mason, I believe," Van Nuys exclaimed cordially. "And is this Mrs. Mason?"

"Miss Street."

"Oh—I beg pardon. Do come in, both of you. You'll excuse the appearance of the room. I was hardly expecting visitors and things are somewhat littered around. Do take that chair, Miss Street, you'll find it very comfortable. I'll get the magazines and newspapers out of it."

The voice was suave, pleasant, well modulated and expressive.

The restless eyes were so black that it was hard to detect expression in them, but his voice more than made up for it. Here was no man who talked in a conversational monotone, but one whose every word seemed alive with expression. His motions as he moved about straightening up the room were graceful, well-timed and effective.

Mason asked jokingly, "Are you this hospitable to *all* your visitors? We might be selling books or soliciting for charitable donations, you know."

Van Nuys smiled cordially. "What if you are, Mr. Mason? You have taken the trouble to come and see me at a rather unconventional hour. I take it that any errand which is important enough to cause that sacrifice of time on your part certainly entitles you to my courteous attention. I'm in the selling game myself, and I always claim anyone is entitled to a respectful hearing."

"Well," Mason admitted, "that's one way of looking at it. You don't know who I am—what I do?"

"No."

"I'm an attorney."

"Mason . . . Mason . . . Not *Perry* Mason."

"That's right."

"Indeed, I've heard of you, Mr. Mason! Daphne told me that you had called."

"Daphne?" Mason asked.

"Mrs. Milfield."

"Oh yes. It's because of her that I'm making this visit."

"Indeed."

"You know her quite well?"

"Oh yes."

"And you knew her husband?"

"Very well indeed, Mr. Mason."

"Then why," Mason asked abruptly, "did she change her mind about flying to San Francisco Friday afternoon?"

Van Nuys was unable to keep expression from his voice although his eyes and face remained a mask. "I'm sorry about that," he said, and his tone showed he was genuinely embarrassed. "I didn't know anyone knew about that."

"May I ask for an explanation?" Mason asked.

"I'm afraid it has absolutely nothing to do with anything in which you're interested, Mr. Mason."

"Meaning that it's none of my business?"

"No, no. Please don't get me wrong on that, Mr. Mason. I . . . I just don't feel free to tell you *all* of the ramifications."

"Why not?"

"Well, to begin with, there's a personal element. I was the one who went to the airport, made her return. And then again it has, in a way, an indirect connection with my friend, who might or might not have given me permission to tell you about it if he had remained alive, but as it is . . . Well, he can't ever give me that permission now."

"You mean Fred Milfield?"

"Yes."

"Why, is it connected with him?"

"Well, it's a domestic problem."

Mason said, "Look here, Van Nuys, I'm not going to beat around the bush. The police are investigating a murder. *They're* not going to leave any stone unturned. *I'm* investigating that same murder, and *I* don't propose to leave any stone unturned."

"May I ask how you happened to know about what took place at the airport?" Van Nuys asked abruptly.

Mason said, "Because *I'm* investigating Milfield's murder, and I think that canceled trip may have some bearing on it."

"It doesn't."

"I'd prefer to be the judge of that."

"You're still not telling me how you knew about it."

"All right. I'm not going to tell you how I knew about it, or how it happens I knew about *your* connection with it. I don't have to."

"I'm sorry, I disagree."

Mason said, "Damn it, I try to tell you in a nice way, and you make me drive it home with a sledge hammer. What I'm *trying* to tell you is that if you don't tell me what it's all about, and give me a satisfactory explanation, then my only recourse is to go to the police and let *them* get the explanation."

"Why?"

"Because I'm representing some people who are interested in having the mystery of Fred Milfield's death cleaned up."

"I'm interested in it myself. If this had any bearing on it, I'd tell you."

"Tell me anyway," Mason said. "I'll decide whether it has any bearing."

Van Nuys glanced at Della Street, uncrossed his knees, then after a moment crossed them again, took a hammered-silver cigarette case from his pocket. "Smoke?" he asked.

"Thanks," Della said.

Mason also took one. They lit up and Mason said, "That business with the cigarette should have given you all the time you needed to think up an explanation."

"It gave me the time," Van Nuys admitted ruefully, "but it hasn't shown me what to do."

"Take your time," Mason said, settling back in the chair.

"All right," Van Nuys blurted. "Do you know anything about Daphne, about her background?"

"Not a thing in the world."

"She's peculiar. She's emotionally unstable."

"What does that mean?"

"She's subject to certain emotional vagaries."

"Are you trying to tell me in a nice way that she's a tramp?" Mason asked.

"No, no—definitely not. She's—she's more of an emotional gypsy."

"And just what is meant by being an emotional gypsy?"

"Well, she's subject to devastating emotional storms. She usually recovers from them quickly. They're short, severe and violent."

"And she's suffering from one at the present time?"

"She *was*."

"An affair with you?"

"With *me!*" Van Nuys laughed. "I'm just a friend of the family. I know her too well, and she knows me too well. I'm only the shoulder she cries on—and that's all I want to be. No, this man was a chap in San Francisco. She had decided to burn her bridges. She had left Fred the usual note that the husband receives under such circumstances, and was about to leave for San Francisco, join her lover and let Fred get a divorce, or do anything else he damn pleased. That's Daphne. She goes completely overboard when she falls. You have to hand it to her for that. She's thorough."

"You speak as though it were a habit."

"Not a habit," Van Nuys said. "It's difficult to explain, Mr. Mason."

"So it would seem."

"Daphne is a woman who has to be violently, madly in love with someone every minute of the time."

"She has a husband," Mason suggested.

"Come, come, Mr. Mason, you're a realist, or you should be. Marriage is a working relationship. It has its moments of genuine, downright boredom. That's the trouble with Daphne. She can't stand being bored. She has to be in love—madly in love, and it's difficult to be madly in love with a husband three hundred and sixty-five days of the year."

"You seem to stick up for her," Mason said.

"I want you to understand her."

"All right, I'll take your word for it. She's an emotional gypsy. She was starting for San Francisco. What did you do?"

"I stopped it."

"Why?"

"Because I knew she'd be more unhappy if she went than if she didn't."

"You caught up with her at the airport and told her she had to come back?"

"That's right."

"So she came back to Los Angeles with you, and you did what?"

"I talked with her. I told her exactly how much of a fool she was about to make of herself."

"And what did she do?"

"Cried at first, then finally agreed with me and told me I was the best friend she'd ever had."

"What time was this?"

"Right after I left the airport."

"You drove her home?"

"Yes."

"How long did it take?"

67

"Twenty to twenty-five minutes."

"How long were you there after you drove her home?"

"About half or three-quarters of an hour."

"How did you know you'd find her at the airport?"

"That's rather a peculiar coincidence."

"Peculiar coincidences are my meat," Mason told him.

"Fred and I have a—*had* a certain business association. We divided up the work."

"You mean you were working with Milfield on this Skinner Hills Karakul Company?"

"In a way, yes. My connection was somewhat indirect."

"What do you mean by that?"

"Well, I was—I was working on other interests than the . . . Oh well, let it go at that, Mr. Mason. There are certain business matters I can't discuss."

"You mean you were working on the oil angle and . . ."

"Now please, Mr. Mason, don't put words in my mouth. All I can say is that I was associated with Fred. He asked me to go to his house and get a brief case containing certain papers. He told me exactly where I would find it. Just in case Daphne *wasn't* home, he gave me his key to the place. He thought that Daphne might be out shopping or something."

"What time was this?" Mason asked.

"Right around noon, a little after."

"Why didn't Milfield get the papers himself?"

"He had an important luncheon engagement."

"And you were to meet him after lunch?"

"No. About four o'clock."

"Do you know where he intended to go then? What he intended to do with the papers?"

"They were papers he wanted to show to Mr. Burbank. Mr. Burbank was expecting him—aboard his yacht."

"But didn't Burbank insist upon absolute privacy on his yacht—refuse to let anyone bother him with business matters?"

"As a rule, yes. This was a very exceptional case. Mr.

Burbank wanted to see Fred. In fact, he'd told him to come to his yacht."

"You're certain?"

"Yes."

"Suppose it should develop that Roger Burbank wasn't aboard the yacht Friday afternoon, and had no intention of being there?"

Van Nuys smiled and shook his head. Both the smile and the gesture were confident. "I think you'll find such is not the case, Mr. Mason."

Mason started to say something, then changed his mind. He gave Van Nuys' answer thoughtful consideration for a few moments, then said, "All right, you went to get the papers. What happened?"

"This note was pinned to a pillow on the davenport."

"What did you do with it—read it and then leave it there?"

"Certainly not. I was afraid Fred might come rushing in. I picked it up and pocketed it."

"The note was meant for Fred?"

"Yes."

"You have that note with you?"

"Really, Mr. Mason, this inquiry is drifting rather far afield, don't you think?"

"No."

"That note, Mr. Mason, affects the happiness of . . ."

"That note," Mason interrupted, "is evidence. At least of an angle of the case that I'm investigating. If you're at all interested in avoiding publicity, I think you will find the best way to do it is to give me the information I'm after."

Van Nuys hesitated for a moment, glanced questioningly at Della Street, and Della, nodding at him, said, "It's the best way. You should be able to see that."

"Oh, all right," Van Nuys surrendered. "Perhaps after all it is best to have the true facts in your possession, Mr. Mason."

He opened a brief case, took out a sheet of paper and handed it to Mason.

It had, Mason observed, been pinned to some cloth. And the double pin hole in the top and the somewhat rumpled appearance of the paper were the natural result of such pinning.

The note was written in pen and ink in a smooth, even handwriting:

Dear Fred:

I know you'll think I'm no good, particularly in view of everything that has gone in the past, but I can't help it. As I've told you a dozen times, I can't control my heart. I can only try to control my emotions. But I simply can't control that peculiar deep-seated something which is perhaps akin to emotion and alive with emotion, yet is far beyond mere emotionalism.

I have debated this step for a long time. I think you will do me the justice to realize that. I think, perhaps, that you have recognized my symptoms, but were afraid to diagnose them, just as I was at first. In short, Fred, I am in love with Doug, and that's all there is to it. It isn't anything you have done, or anything you have failed to do. Nor is there anything either of us can do now. You have been wonderful to me, and I shall always admire and respect you. I will admit that I got lonely during the last four or five weeks when it seemed every minute of your time, day and night, was taken up with this oil deal. But I know how those things are, and realize that you're doing a splendid job and are in a position to make a lot of money. My congratulations to you. Needless to say, Fred, I won't want a cent. You can go ahead with divorce proceedings and make out a waiver, or property settlement, or whatever it is you have to make out under such circumstances. Your lawyer will tell you. I hope we can always be friends. Good-by, Dear.

Yours,

DAPHNE

"A nice note," Mason said.

"She meant it—meant every word of it," Van Nuys said.

"I dare say she did. Who's Doug?"

"The man she was going to meet in San Francisco."

"How delightfully definite! What's the rest of his name?"

Van Nuys smiled and shook his head, "Really, Mr. Mason, there *is* a limit, you know."

"Limit to what?"

"Limit to how far we can go in dragging others into this thing."

"Oh bosh! You're in a murder case now. Who's Doug?"

"I'm afraid I'm not at liberty to give you that information." Van Nuys was formal and dignified now.

Mason abruptly pushed back his chair and got to his feet. "All right, Van Nuys, thanks for what you've given me."

"Can I trust you to keep it confidential?"

"Not in the least."

"I understood you were going to."

"Then you misunderstood me."

"I thought you said that the alternative was that you'd give the information to the police."

"That's absolutely correct."

"You're not going to give it to them?"

"Certainly I'm going to give it to them. The only thing that would prevent me from doing so would be a very definite feeling that there was some reason why I shouldn't."

"I tell you all of this has absolutely nothing to do with Fred's death. That's a matter between him and—well, between him and someone else."

"You say this man's in San Francisco?"

"Yes."

"Has he ever written her?"

Van Nuys avoided Mason's eyes.

Mason said, "Phooey! The police will smoke all this out. There's no mystery about it. They'll ask her to account for all her motions Friday afternoon. If she lies, she'll put herself in an awful mess."

"There are no letters the police will ever find," Van Nuys said.

"You mean they've been destroyed?"

"I mean the police will never find them."

Abruptly Mason reached over and took possession of the brief case that Van Nuys had placed by the side of his chair. "You mean," he said, "that you have them?"

"Mr. Mason, please! That's *my* brief case."

Mason said to Della Street, "Call Lieutenant Tragg."

There was a moment of tense silence. Della got up and moved toward the telephone.

Van Nuys waited until she had picked up the receiver, then he said suddenly, "Hang up the phone, Miss Street. The letters are in the right-hand compartment of the brief case, Mr. Mason."

Della hung up the telephone. Mason opened the brief case, took out the letters, glanced at them, thrust them in his pocket.

"What are you going to do with those?" Van Nuys asked in alarm.

"I'm going to study them," Mason said, "and if your contention seems to be correct and they aren't connected with the case, I'm going to give them back to you."

"Otherwise?" Van Nuys asked.

"Otherwise," Mason said, "I'm going to keep them."

Mason started for the door, paused, said, "So when you found this note you rushed to the airport."

"Yes."

"Without keeping your appointment with Milfield?"

"No. I took him the papers he wanted, and *then* rushed to the airport."

"Where did you meet him?"

"Out in front of this hotel. He was in a hurry to leave for the yacht club. He was half an hour late. He was in something of an emotional state."

"Over what?"

"Some business problem. He said someone had been lying about him."

"Lies that had been told to Burbank?"

"So I understood. However, I had too much on my own mind to ask for particulars just then. Fred was in a hurry because he was late and was afraid he was going to miss meeting Burbank.—That's a point on which you seem to be in error, Mr. Mason. Burbank and Milfield had a five o'clock appointment at the yacht club. Burbank was going to bring his dinghy with the outboard motor in to the mooring float at exactly five o'clock."

"I see. So you had to wait here at the hotel for half an hour before Milfield showed up?"

"That's right—thirty-five minutes to be exact. I stood out in front, waiting."

"What made him late?"

"I don't know. He was terribly worked up."

"And Mrs. Milfield was still at the airport when you got there?"

"Fortunately yes. She hadn't been able to secure a ticket. She'd waited on a stand-by arrangement whereby they'd assign her the first vacant seat in case of a last minute cancellation."

"So you drove her back?"

"Yes."

"Showed her the note you'd found?"

"Yes, of course."

Mason said, "I'll want to think this over a bit."

Van Nuys said with dignity, "I'm sorry, Mr. Mason, that you can't seem to see Mrs. Milfield as I see her."

Mason said, "I'm going to do a little thinking about her."

"And I don't think you've really tried to," Van Nuys said.

"Perhaps I haven't," Mason admitted. "I don't want to see people as other people see them, I want to see them as *I* see them. Good night."

9

■

While they were waiting for the elevator, Mason said to Della Street, "Now then, I'm going to drive you home, and you're going to sleep."

She laughed. "Don't be silly."

"You're all in."

"All in nothing! If you think you can hold out whatever's in those letters, you have another guess coming."

Mason grinned. "Want to devour all the purple passages?"

"Every one of them," she admitted. "After all, don't you make allowances for feminine curiosity?"

"I'm trying to make allowances for feminine fatigue."

"I haven't any, any more. That dinner made me feel ever so much better and—gosh, Chief, I could sit and listen to Van Nuys talk all night."

"A very remarkable voice," Mason admitted. "It probably indicates rather a remarkable personality."

"A woman's fortunate to have a friend like that," Della said wistfully. "Someone who really understands her and sympathizes with her and—and tries to save her."

"Save her from what?" Mason asked.

"From herself, of course."

"Daphne Milfield evidently didn't want to be saved from herself."

"Of course she didn't. But I mean it's splendid for her

to have a friend like Harry Van Nuys. When are you going to read those letters, Chief?"

Mason grinned. "Tomorrow morning."

They walked across the lobby of the hotel.

"Good night," Mason said to the clerk.

His response was an all but inarticulate grunt.

"Come on, Chief, where are you going to read them?"

"In the office, of course."

"When?"

"Tomorrow morning."

She laughed. "Fat chance. Come on, we'll turn on the dash light in the automobile."

They sat side by side in the automobile. There were half a dozen letters, all written in pen and ink. Those which bore the earlier postmarks had the return address of Douglas Burwell at a San Francisco hotel. Those that had been written later simply had the initials D. B., and the address of the San Francisco hotel as a return. The letters covered a period of some six weeks and indicated a progressive intimacy.

"Well?" Mason asked Della Street when they had finished reading them.

"He sounds like a nice boy," Della said.

"A boy?"

"Well, he's—sort of inexperienced in that sort of thing."

"What makes you think so?"

"Just the way he's gone about it. The . . . Oh, I don't know. He's fallen head over heels, and that's all there is to it. He's naïve, and an idealist. He'd never be happy with her. Van Nuys was right. It would have been a great tragedy."

"Well," Mason said, "let's see what he has to say for himself."

"What do you mean?"

"We're going to call him on long distance. There's no time to get up there for an interview. And even then, an interview might be wasted. Let's beat the police to the punch and see what Mr. Douglas Burwell has to say for himself."

They called him from a long distance booth in one of the larger hotels, and at that hour the call was put through with such rapidity that within a matter of seconds, the operator made her report. "Mr. Mason, on your call to Douglas Burwell—he is out of town for a few days."

"Do you know where he could be reached by telephone?" Mason asked.

The girl said sweetly, "You may talk with the clerk at the hotel, if you wish. All the information we can give is that he's out of town."

"Very well," Mason said, and then over his shoulder to Della Street, "I'll bet he's in Los Angeles. What'll you bet, Della?"

A moment later a masculine voice said, "Hello."

Mason said, "I'm trying to get in touch with Douglas Burwell. It's very important."

"You are in Los Angeles, aren't you?"

"Yes."

"Well, he's there."

"Can you tell me where I can reach him?"

"At the Hotel Claymore."

"Thank you," Mason said, and hung up.

"Now then," Mason said to Della Street, "one thing is definite and certain. *You* are going home and go to bed."

"What did they say about Burwell?"

"He's here in Los Angeles."

"Where?"

"At the Claymore Hotel."

"It's not over two blocks," Della said, and then added as Mason hesitated, "and if I go home in the middle of all this, I won't sleep anyway."

"You should learn not to get so excited over a murder," Mason told her.

"Murder my eye! This is romance. That's something entirely different. Come on, Chief, let's go."

10

Douglas Burwell proved to be a tall man, about thirty, prominent cheekbones, large, limpid dark eyes, and a somewhat tubercular appearance, with dark wavy hair. There were circles under his eyes. His hair was rumpled in disarray, and the ash tray on the table beside the most comfortable chair in the room was filled to overflowing with cigarettes, none of which seemed to have been smoked to more than half its length.

His voice showed the emotional tension under which he was laboring, and his manner had none of the cordial hospitality which had characterized Harry Van Nuys.

"Well, what is it?" he demanded shortly.

Mason, giving him the benefit of a searching glance, lashed out without any preliminaries, "I want to ask you some questions about Mrs. Milfield."

If Mason had, without warning, struck the man in the stomach, his reactions could not have indicated any greater dismay or surprise. "About . . . about . . ."

"About Mrs. Milfield," Mason said, kicking the door shut and indicating the comfortable chair. "Sit down, Della."

"But I don't know anything about Mrs. Milfield."

"Know Fred Milfield?" Mason asked.

"I have met him, yes."

"Business?"

"Yes."

"When did you meet his wife?"

"I . . . why, I think I only met her once, Mr. . . . What did you say your name was?"

"Mason."

"I only met her once, Mr. Mason. And may I ask the reason for all of this? I don't appreciate your barging into my room and throwing questions like this at me. Are you connected with the police?"

"You heard her husband had been murdered?"

"Yes."

"How did you know he was murdered?"

"She told me."

"Oh, you've seen her then?"

His voice was cautious now, and dignified. "I rang up the house to try and get in touch with Mr. Milfield. She told me what had happened."

"That was the only reason you rang up the house?"

"Yes."

"And you aren't particularly friendly with his wife?"

"Mr. Mason, I tell you I've only seen the woman once. She impressed me as being a very attractive woman, but for the life of me, I couldn't describe her to you. She went in one eye and out the other."

Mason said, "That's fine. That gives me a perfect case."

"What do you mean?" Burwell asked.

Mason said, "You have a good action against someone and I want to represent you in that action."

"You're an attorney?"

"Yes."

"Oh. I thought you were connected with the police."

"Not directly," Mason said. "But the police will naturally expect you to take some action and I'm in a position to represent you."

"Take some action! What do you mean?"

"In the prosecution for forgery."

"Prosecuting whom for forgery?"

Mason reached in his pocket and pulled out the stack of six letters. "The person," he said, "who forged your name to these letters. The person who wrote these very interesting, somewhat naïve and rather passionate letters to Mrs. Fred Milfield and signed your name to them."

Resistance oozed out of Burwell as air from a punctured tire. "My letters!" he exclaimed.

"*Your* letters?"

"Yes."

"I thought you said you hardly knew the woman."

"Mr. Mason, *where* did you get those letters?"

"Does that need to enter into it?"

"Yes."

"They were given to me," Mason said.

"By whom?"

"It might have been the police," Mason said, "or it might have been a newspaper reporter, or it might have been a client. I can't tell you where I received them. But I *can* tell you what I'm going to do with them."

"What?"

"I'm going to give them to the police."

"Mr. Mason, *please* don't do that."

"Why not?"

"The newspapers would get hold of them."

"I can't help that. I have no right to keep evidence from the police."

"Evidence!"

"Yes."

"Of what?"

"Evidence connecting you with the murder of Fred Milfield."

"Mr. Mason, are you stark, staring crazy?"

"I don't think so."

"What possible connection do those letters have . . . ?"

Mason said, "Listen, Burwell, why don't you come clean? Mrs. Milfield was on her way to San Francisco to join you. She was going to run away with you. She was stopped by a friend. She . . ."

"It was a friend who stopped her!" Burwell exclaimed.

Mason nodded.

"No. That wasn't it. She just changed her mind. She told me over the telephone that she'd decided not to come. She . . . Mr. Mason, this isn't another trap. You're not trying to trap me, are you?"

Mason indicated the telephone, "Ring her up and ask her."

Burwell started toward the telephone, then changed his mind. "No, I . . . No, I won't do that . . . not now."

"All right," Mason said, "do it later then. She started to go to San Francisco. A friend of her husband made her change her mind, and so you came down here. And Fred Milfield had found out about the whole affair. He was aboard Burbank's yacht. You were just young enough and crazy enough to go down there to see him. You two men had it out, and he made a swing at you. You hit him, and . . ."

"Stop!" Burwell exclaimed. "You have absolutely no grounds for making any such statement. Fred Milfield was nothing in my life. I had no reason to see him. I didn't want to see him. He was a hard, tyrannical husband. He was absolutely callous to the emotional needs of his wife. He left her completely starved for affection while he devoted himself to the everlasting pursuit of the almighty dollar. He wasn't worthy to touch the hem of her garment. He wasn't . . ."

Mason said, "You've been reading the old-fashioned romances. Why don't you get yourself up to date?"

There was misery in Burwell's eyes.

"All right," Mason said, taking sympathy on the man's quite evident distress, "you came to Los Angeles. You got in touch with Mrs. Milfield. What did she say?"

"She told me . . ."

"Yes?" Mason asked.

"Well," Burwell blurted, "she told me her husband had been killed, and that I mustn't try to see her because the police would become suspicious."

"And what time was this?" Mason asked.

"Shortly after I got off the train."

Mason veiled his glance at Della Street, said rather unconcernedly, "You came down on the Lark, didn't you?"

"That's right."

"Did you call her from the depot or from the hotel?"

"From my hotel."

"About what time?"

"Oh, somewhere right around ten o'clock."

"I see," Mason said very carelessly. "And she told you her husband had been murdered?"

"Not then. I couldn't get her on the phone when I first called."

Mason slipped the letters back into his pocket. "You got her later?"

"Yes. When I finally got hold of her, she told me about her husband's death."

"Told you he had been murdered?"

"Well, not in so many words. She said there'd been an unfortunate accident and he had been killed, and that the police were investigating."

"What did she tell you to do?"

"Told me to keep away from the place, to make no effort to see her, and to take the next train back to San Francisco."

"And you didn't do that?"

"No."

"You came down on the Lark?" Mason asked.

"That's right."

"And as I understand your story, you called Mrs. Milfield as soon as you got to town?"

"I tried to call her, yes. She didn't answer until shortly after noon."

"Shortly after noon, eh," Mason said somewhat musingly. "You don't think it was as late as one o'clock?"

"Oh, no. It was right around noon sometime."

Mason glanced at Della Street and said very casually, "That was the first you had heard about it?"

"Yes."

"And she told you some of the details?"

"She said the body had been found on Mr. Burbank's yacht, and that I wasn't to say anything about it."

"You didn't go back to San Francisco?"

"Certainly not. I want to be here. I want to be near her in case there's anything I can do to help, in case . . ."

"There isn't," Mason interrupted.

"Oh, I know! My reason tells me that's the case; but I can't bring myself to leave."

"You keep hoping you may have a chance to see her, don't you?"

"Well, yes."

"Did you," Mason asked, "know Roger Burbank?"

"No."

Mason said, "I may get in touch with you again. In the meantime, if I were you, I'd make no attempt to communicate with Mrs. Milfield in any way."

"Mr. Mason, can't you tell me how she is? Can't you tell me how she's looking—how she's standing up? This is a terrific strain. This is . . ."

Mason interrupted him to say, "Do you get talkative when you get drunk?"

Burwell laughed nervously, "No. I get dizzy and go to sleep." There was something almost apologetic in the statement.

Mason held the door open for Della Street. "My advice to you then," he said, his voice firm to the point of command, "is to start in without delay and get yourself quite drunk. Good night."

11

■

The Skinner Hills lay in rolling contours under a warm California sun. The early spring grass gave them a soft green texture that made the land seem fertile and prosperous.

A month or so later, when the dry season had become definitely established, the sun would toast the hills to a golden brown. Then the beauty spots would be the massive live oaks which would furnish relief from the glare of the eye-aching sunlight. Now those trees which dotted the green landscape were mere incidentals. The eye feasted upon the rolling green slopes.

Mason stopped his car on a turn in the road at the summit of the grade, and said to Della Street, "Well, here you are."

"How beautiful!" she exclaimed.

"It is," Mason agreed.

"Where are all these Karakul sheep?"

Mason took binoculars from the glove compartment, opened the car door and got out to stand in the warm, late, spring sunlight, his elbow propped against the door to steady the binoculars.

"There they are."

"You mean those little spots way down there in the pasture?"

"Yes."

"Let me look."

Della Street swung quickly in a half turn, thrust out her feet, jumped to the ground with a swirl of skirts, then came to stand at Mason's side. The lawyer handed her the binoculars, moved over so that she could rest her arm on the door of the car.

"Oh, how interesting!" Della Street exclaimed, looking through the powerful glasses. "So *that's* where our fur coats come from?"

"That's right."

"You mean those sheep make . . ."

"Not the mature sheep. The hair from the mature sheep makes tweed clothing, blankets, rugs and that sort of stuff. Karakul coats are made from one day old, newborn lambs."

"Seems a mean trick to play on the lambs," Della said.

"It is."

"I never knew that before."

"On the other hand," Mason said, "if it weren't for the fur industry, the strain wouldn't be cultivated, so the lamb wouldn't be born at all—so there you are."

"Something like which came first, the chicken or the egg."

"Exactly."

"And just what do you propose to do?"

Mason said, "I'm going to find this man, Frank Palermo, and see just what he knows—if he'll talk. And then we're going to have a nice, friendly session with our clients."

Della said, "You think your clients are holding out on you?"

Mason indicated the winding road. "If what Van Nuys says is true, they are. According to my information, we turn off there to the left and take the road that winds over toward that range of brushy hills."

Della handed the binoculars back to Mason, who put them in their leather case. They got back into the automobile and Mason drove down the winding grade.

They crossed over a little gully on a short bridge. The

road started climbing. Mason gunned the car up the long rolling slopes, then abruptly turned to the left on a dirt road.

"Fresh car tracks on this road," Della said. "It looks as though it had quite a bit of use."

"Uh huh."

"Do you know what Palermo looks like?" Della asked.

"I know his type."

"What's it like?"

"Bullheaded, obstinate, cunning, two-fisted, glittering eyes, an overbearing manner, and a breath that is composed of one part garlic, one part sour wine."

Della laughed. "You make him sound very hard-boiled."

"Probably not doing him justice even yet. He's just the type you'd like to have discover corpses in cases the other fellow is handling."

For several miles now they had been passing little shack houses, unpainted cabins with stovepipes thrust out through terra cotta rings serving as chimneys, desolate, weather-beaten, deserted cabins that bore silent witness to man's struggle with the poverty of poor land. Now, thanks to the purchasing activities of Fred Milfield and the Skinner Hills Karakul Fur Company, the owners of this land had sold out at attractive prices and had moved away, basking in comparative affluence.

The dirt road topped a ridge, descended into a little canyon. Ahead of them was a cabin typical of all the other cabins save that a faint wisp of smoke was coming from the chimney.

"Probably cooking his Sunday dinner," Mason explained to Della Street.

"Is this the place?"

"According to my sketch map, this is it."

Mason drove the car across a dry wash, spurted up the incline on the other side, rounded a wooded knoll and turned into the refuse-littered yard around the cabin.

Immediately back of this cabin were the high hills which

marked the end of the rolling sheep country. These hills were thickly covered with chamiso and scrub oak interspersed with clumps of grayish-green sage.

The door of the cabin was flung open. A thick-chested, florid-faced man with a shock of iron-gray hair stood in the doorway. His grayish-green eyes glittered with the effort of concentration.

"I'm looking for Frank Palermo."

"All right. You come to right place. This, he is Frank Palermo. What you want?"

"I am Perry Mason, the lawyer."

A sudden surge of enthusiasm flooded the man's face. He came running forward, hand outstretched. "Mist' Mason! By Gar—beeg lawyer like you come to see little sheepherder like me. Son-of-a-gun! I bet you that car cost plenty money, huh? Jiz' get out. Bringa da lady. We make good talk—you and me. We have a good glass of vino, no?"

"No," Mason said, grinning at Della Street. "We have to talk right here. I'm in a hurry." He got out of the car, shook hands.

"But you have glass of vino, eh? I bring heem out."

"Sorry," Mason said, "but I never drink before noon."

Palermo's face fell. "I got some ver' fine vino—kind you don't get in no restaurant. Restaurant wine he's too sweet. Iss not good for you drink sweet wine like that. Drink good sour wine that make you strong, no?"

"It's all right if you're accustomed to it," Mason said. "If you're not, it's a pretty strong drink."

"Not strong at all. Who's the lady? Thata your wife?"

"That's my secretary."

"Your secretay, huh! Whatcha do with secretay?"

Mason's eyes were smiling. "She writes down things that are said."

Della Street gave Palermo a smile.

Palermo's eyes twinkled with the lusty appreciation of one man of the world talking to another in a cryptic language which only they can understand. "By jiz' that's something! She writes things down, huh?" And Palermo threw back his head and laughed uproariously.

Della Street surreptitiously reached in the glove compartment of the car, took out a shorthand notebook and a pencil, held the notebook on her lap where Palermo couldn't see it, her pencil poised over it. She said to Mason, "Your description seems to have been pretty accurate. How's the halitosis, did you hit the nail on the head on that? I'm out of range."

Mason said, "You're fortunate. If I can manipulate you into a position of proximity, your olfactory nerves will acclaim me a prophet."

Palermo ceased laughing instantly, his bushy eyebrows pulled down in a scowl over his glittering little eyes as they switched back and forth from Mason to Della Street. "Whatsa that you say?" he asked.

"My secretary was reminding me," Mason said, "that I have an appointment late this afternoon, and I'll have to be getting back to my office."

"Jiz' you work Sundays?"

"Sometimes."

Palermo's eyes shifted to the car. "You make lotsa money. Why you work on Sundays?"

"I make so much money," Mason explained gravely, "that I have to work Sundays to pay my income tax."

"By Gar! You make so much money—you not make enough for tax! By Gar, that's tough. Iss plenty tough! Look, I got the idea, we make lots the money. I want to see you, by Gar, and now you come see me."

"You wanted to see me about the land?"

"Sure about the land. What you think? You get your people file a lawsuit against me, huh? Then we all get rich."

"How?" Mason asked.

"You prove I no got title to land, huh?"

"You haven't any title, Palermo."

"No, no! I mean you do it the way I tell you. We fix it up. I help prove I no got the title."

"You mean you'll deliberately lose the lawsuit?"

Palermo's head nodded vigorously, his eyes were sharp and glittering. "That's right."

"Why?" Mason asked.

Palermo unconsciously reached out for Mason's arm once more, trying to draw him away from the automobile.

"Just *how*?" Mason asked.

"We make money outa sheep—outa fur sheep for ladies' coats," Palermo said, and then again roared with laughter, giving Mason a quick dig in the ribs. "You betcha we make money outa da fur sheep."

Mason waited.

Palermo lowered his voice to little more than a garlic-coated whisper, leaned close to Mason, "You know something? I give Milfield contract to buy my property for— well, for plenty money."

"But you don't have the title to that eighty-acre tract."

"Poof! I get title all right. Don't you worry none about me. Frank Palermo, he smart man. You a lawyer, but I know law pretty good myself too, maybe—huh? Five years I stay on that property and I pay taxes. After that can't do nothing, no. I see that in court once. My brother, he do the same thing. I come here, I decide I'm going to be smart like my brother."

"This time," Mason said, "you were *too* smart."

For a moment there was antagonism in the little deep-set eyes, then Palermo was once more vociferously friendly. "Look, Mist' Mason, you know what happen? Day before yesterday a man comes to my place—he's got big car like yours. He says, 'Palermo, how much money Mr. Milfield he going to give you for property?'

"I say, 'Why you want to know?' He say, 'Because maybe I give you more.'

"'All right,' I tell him. I say, 'I make a contract—one price in the contract. But Milfield, he gives me money for cash. I put in my pocket. That money, nothing said about in the contract.' "

"Did you tell him how much that money was?" Mason asked.

"Sure I tell him. He's one thousand dollars—one thousand dollars for cash. But the contract, he don't say nothing about the one thousand dollars in cash. Then Milfield shows that contract to other men got the property around here and makes look all right, see?"

Mason nodded.

"All right, this man he says, 'Look, maybe I can get you *five* thousand dollars for your property.'—You get that? Five thousand dollars! Jiz' whata break! Already I've signed my name on contract. But I don't think contract he's good."

"Why not?" Mason asked.

"Is no witness."

"But you signed your name?"

"Sure I sign my name—what the hell, why not sign my name? I get one thousand dollars cash money when I sign my name—why not?"

"Then as I get it," Mason said, "you want me to file suit against you so it will be determined that you have no title?"

The little eyes sparkled with appreciation. "That's right."

"And have you put off the property?"

The head nodded vigorously.

"And then," Mason asked, "what do we do?"

"Jiz'! what do we do? Then I can't sell to Milfield because I got no title, see? He don't get back no one thousand dollars because no witness. I say by Gar, he never pay no thousand dollars. Only price he to pay is on contract and no witness. All right. You get property. I not got the property. Then I can't sell. Then contract he's no good because I got no property. You got the property. You sell this man for five thousand dollars. You take one-

90

half for you, one-half for me. We all make money, No?"

Palermo was peering anxiously at Mason, trying to see how the lawyer would react to his proposition.

Mason said, "I don't think my client would be interested. What was the name of this man who was out here?"

"By Gar, he don't want tell me any name. He says his name come later. But I'm smart. When he's not look, I write down license of his automobile—big automobile like yours. Fine car. I get license number. What the hell you care what man tells you about his name when you got license number, huh?"

"This was Friday?" Mason asked.

"Friday, yes."

"What time?"

"In afternoon."

"What time in the afternoon?"

"I don't know. I don't carry no watch. Just a little in afternoon. You see that tree? The shadow that tree when this man comes, is right here."

Palermo walked rapidly over to a point some forty feet south of the trunk of a live oak tree. He dug with his heel into the ground, leaving a little furrow of turned up soil. "Right here," he said. "The shadow is right here."

Mason noticed the tree and the angle of the sun and nodded. "And you have the license number of his car?"

"Sure I get his number. I get pencil and write down number of automobile. I'm smart man myself. You smart lawyer. I am smart sheep man. You get that property. You sell it quick for five thousand dollars. We split fifty-fifty."

"And," Mason asked, flashing a quick glance at Della Street, "do we also split the thousand dollars you got in cash from Milfield?"

Palermo drew back. "Say! What the hell you talk about? I never got it. Is no witness."

Mason laughed.

Palermo pushed stubby fingers down into his watch pocket, pulled out a folded bit of paper. On it had been scrawled the rambling figures so characteristic of the writing of a man who is all but illiterate. He read out the license number, 8P3035.

Mason smiled, shook his head. "I'm not here to talk about your property claim, Palermo. I want you to see a lawyer about that. I came to ask you about what happened Saturday morning."

The little suspicious eyes narrowed. "Saturday morning! Is nothing. I go aboard yacht to see Milfield. Is dead. That's all."

"How did you know that Milfield was to be aboard that yacht?"

"Because I know he's there."

"How did you know he's there?"

"Because he tell me is going to be there."

"You telephoned Milfield!"

"That's right."

"Did you tell him about this other man having been to see you?"

"Sure I tell him."

"And what did Milfield say?"

"Milfield he say to come see him tomorrow on yacht. Is all excited quick."

"Look here," Mason said. "If you were to meet Milfield Saturday morning on that yacht, you must have had some sort of a deal fixed up."

Palermo threw out his hands in a little gesture of disclaimer. "What the hell? You can't get money from man who is dead. I know that. No writing, is no good. Lawyer tell my brother all about that."

"So you did have some agreement with Milfield?" Mason asked. "Some understanding you'd reached over the telephone, something that would have worked out all right if Milfield had lived?"

"Is no witness," Palermo said doggedly.

"All right, you went out to the yacht. What did you find?"

"I find yacht all right. I've got the name from that yacht written down on piece of paper, see? I scull out. I find the yacht. All right, I go around in boat. Me, I am pretty good boatman. I look at that yacht quick. I see is no way to get ashore from that yacht."

"What do you mean?"

"No boat. No skiff. Just yacht. How you going to get to shore from yacht with no boat, huh? All right, to myself, I say 'Little boat is gone. That means men aboard yacht are gone. That means Frank Palermo he come all the way for nothing.' Me, I am sore. I yelled. Nobody answer. All right, I get aboard."

"The yacht was at anchor?" Mason asked.

Palermo laughed. "The yacht she is stuck in the mud. Can't go no place when yacht stuck in mud."

"But there was water all around it?"

"Oh, sure. Water, but not enough."

"You are in your own boat?"

"Sure, in my own boat. Right there is boat, all folded up. I take hunters out on lake in that boat. You think I am going to pay rent for boat when already I have boat? What the hell? You think I am crazy, me, Frank Palermo?"

"I was just wondering about the boat," Mason explained.

"All right. Now you know. Is my own boat."

"And what did you do?"

"I go down the stairs."

"Was the hatch pushed back?"

"Hatch is pushed back."

"And what did you find?"

"First I don't find nothing. Then I look around, I see dead man. Is Milfield. Idea comes to my mind like one flash. 'All right, Milfield is dead, so then is no witness. Contract is no good without witness.'"

"Where was Milfield lying?"

"Over against the side of cabin."

"Against the low side?"

"Sure."

93

"The yacht was tilted over?"

"Sure, is low tide."

"What did you do?"

"Get out fast."

"Did you touch anything?"

Palermo grinned. "Only my feet. I am not damn fool."

"Perhaps you touched the top of the hatch when you went down into the cabin."

"Sure."

"You left fingerprints there?"

"Well, what of it? That was in the morning. Man is dead already for all night."

"But you may have left fingerprints?"

Palermo raised his voice. "Say, what's the matter? Maybe you like to make trap for me and take all that five thousand, huh? What you mean maybe fingerprints?"

Mason said, "I'm trying to find out . . ."

"You try to find out too damn much! Whatsa matter you don't make a deal with me? Maybe you try get rope around *my* neck so you get property, huh?"

Palermo turned abruptly and stalked toward his cabin.

Mason said, "I simply wanted to ask you . . ."

Palermo whirled, his face was dark with rage. "You get the hell off my property," he shouted. "When I get to cabin, I get shotgun."

Mason watched the man turn and plunge along toward his cabin.

"I think, Chief," Della Street said, "you've obtained *just* about all the information you are going to get."

Mason nodded, said nothing, stood watching the cabin, saw Palermo pull the screen door to one side, enter the cabin, slam the door behind him.

"Better get started before he comes out with that shotgun," Della urged. "He's just about half crazy."

Mason said, "Just as a psychological experiment, Della, I'd like to see whether he *does* bring out a gun."

"Chief, I'm nervous."

"So am I," Mason admitted, grinning.

"He doesn't seem to be coming out."

Mason waited another thirty seconds, then slowly walked along the car, opened the door and slid in behind the steering wheel.

Della Street switched on the ignition.

"Do you want to ring up Paul Drake about that license number?" she asked, glancing apprehensively toward the cabin.

Mason's lips tightened. "That," he said, "isn't going to be necessary. I happened to recognize the license number."

"You did! Whose car is it?"

"The car," Mason said, "is the one in which I was given such an interesting ride yesterday afternoon. The one in which Carol Burbank took me up to the Surf and Sun Motel and subsequently back to the little 'dobe restaurant."

12

■

It was late afternoon when Della Street and Perry Mason emerged from the elevator and walked down the long corridor. As they went past Paul Drake's office, Mason opened the door, thrust his head in and said to the girl at the switchboard, "Drake in?"

"Yes. He's waiting."

"Ask him to come down to my office. What are *you* doing at the switchboard? I thought this was your day off."

"The girl who takes care of the board Saturdays and Sundays is laid up with the flu," she said, "so I'm having to work right on through," and she made a little grimace. "However, Mr. Drake says I can get off next week for . . . Here he is now."

The door from one of the inner offices opened and Drake, talking in his characteristic drawl, said, "Hi, Perry. Thought I heard your voice. Hello, Della. Want to talk now?"

"Uh huh."

"Okay, I'll come on down with you. I'll be in Mr. Mason's office if anything turns up, Frances. You have the unlisted number, haven't you?"

"Yes."

"Hold everything, except on this stuff I'm doing for Mason; put that on through to me."

Drake moved over to take Della's arm. "Why don't you

work for a *good* outfit?" he asked. "We keep *our* girls on a five-day week, a seven-hour day."

"Yes, I notice. Frances was just telling us."

Drake laughed and said, "You can't win!"

Mason opened the door of his office.

Drake said, "There's something new on that murder, Perry. Remember that doorway to the after cabin on the yacht? It was shown in those pictures."

"Yes, I remember. What about it?"

"The autopsy surgeon thinks that Milfield *may* have received the fatal injury by being knocked over against the raised brass-covered threshold between the main cabin and a smaller private cabin."

"In other words, he may have met his death as the result of a fist fight? That would change it from first-degree murder to manslaughter."

"That, of course, will be up to a jury. Police will go ahead on the first-degree murder theory. You understand this other thing is just a possibility, Perry. It . . ."

The phone on Mason's desk rang sharply. Mason said, "Better answer it, Paul. It's probably Frances relaying some information."

Drake took the telephone, said, "Hello," then listened carefully for nearly two minutes, made a couple of notes, said, "Okay. Tell him to wait right there at that telephone for five minutes."

Drake hung up, said, "We've located J. C. Lassing, the man who rented that double cabin at the Surf and Sun Motel. My operative says he's got the guy parked outside the drugstore where he's calling. He thinks Lassing will give him a written statement."

Mason showed excitement. "What does he say?"

Drake said, "J. C. Lassing lives at 6842 La Brea Avenue, Colton. It was a little job tracing him because he'd transposed two of the figures on his license number when he registered at the motel. Lots of people do that; even when they're looking right at a figure, they'll transpose a couple of the digits in writing it down, and when they're trying to remember a license number . . ."

Mason said, "I know."

"What I'm getting at," Drake pointed out, "is that it *may* have been accidental that he gave the wrong figure. Again, it may not. Anyhow, he just about corroborates Burbank's story. He says he rented two double cabins; that there were four people in his party, and that he 'believes there were subsequently two more people who arrived.' He won't tell the names of any of them."

"You say your man can get a written statement from him?"

"He thinks he can. He has Lassing waiting outside in his car. There's one thing that bothers me though, and that's why he rang up before he tried to get a statement. Lassing mentioned casually that his party checked out right after noon Saturday. That wouldn't fit in with your time theory, would it, Perry?"

Mason said, "No. Burbank apparently didn't leave until around four or five o'clock in the afternoon. Get your man on the phone, Paul, tell him to ask Lassing more about that time element."

Drake dialed his office on the telephone, said, "Ring up Al, Frances, tell him that he's to find out more about that checking out time before he tries to get the written statement out of Lassing. Have him call back as soon as he finds out."

Drake hung up the telephone and turned to Mason. He had only started to say something when the phone rang again.

Della answered the phone, said, "Yes. . . . Yes, this is Miss Street. . . . Just a moment. Hold the phone."

She placed her hand over the mouthpiece, said to Mason, "It's Carol. She's at the Union Terminal; wants to know if you've found out anything."

Mason made a gesture of impatience. "Tell her we're waiting for an important call. Tell her to wait right there.

Get a number where we can call her back. As soon as we can clear the line, I want to ask her where her father is and what he was doing calling on Frank Palermo Friday afternoon. Don't tell her that. Just get a number where we can call her and get her off the line."

Della relayed the message, hung up.

They waited in tense silence for less than a minute, then the phone rang again. Della answered it, said, "Just a minute, Frances," and passed the phone over to Paul Drake.

Drake said, "Hello. . . . Yes, Frances. . . . The devil! . . . Look, can you work the switchboard so as to put him on the line? It'll save time. . . . All right, do it. . . . Oh, hello, Al. . . . That's what Frances told me. . . . Tell me exactly what happened."

There was an interval of silence. Then Drake said, "Just a minute, I'll pass that on. You hold the phone."

He turned to Mason: "Al says he left Lassing out in his car while he put through the call to me. You heard me tell him to stick around the telephone for five minutes, so he waited right there. Then when Frances called him back and told him to go ask Lassing about that time element, he went out. Lassing wasn't there."

"Skipped out?" Mason rasped.

"No, the cops nabbed him."

"Is Al sure?"

"Yes. A kid told Al some men came up in a car that had a red spotlight on it and a star on the side door. One of the men got out and went over and started talking with Lassing, and then, all of a sudden, he pulled out a pair of handcuffs, put them on Lassing and . . ."

"Handcuffs!" Mason interrupted.

"That's what Al says the kid told him."

Mason said, "Tell Al to get out of there, fast!"

Drake said into the telephone, "Okay, Al, come on back to the office—step on it," and hung up the phone.

Mason, pacing the floor, quickened the tempo of his stride.

Drake said, "I can't figure what . . ."

"Wait a minute," Mason interrupted, his voice sharp with nervous tension. "Let me think."

For two or three minutes he paced up and down the office, then he suddenly whirled to Paul Drake, "Got a good woman operative, Paul—one you can trust?"

Drake said, "What for, rough stuff, siren stuff or . . ."

"No, someone who can stay with a high-class woman every minute of the time, not let her out of her sight day or night."

"I know a girl like that. It'll take me a while to get her lined up," Drake said.

"How long?"

"Oh, four or five hours maybe, perhaps sooner."

Mason shook his head. "We've got to do something before then, Paul."

Drake said dubiously, "I have a woman who used to . . . No, Perry, I don't think she'll do."

Mason said, "Damn it, we haven't got all night!"

"Can I do it?" Della Street asked.

Mason turned to contemplate her thoughtfully. "Yes," he said, "you can do it—and I guess you'll have to do it."

"What is it?"

Mason said, "When you leave here be damn certain you aren't followed. Get on and get off streetcars, then grab yourself a taxicab. Tell the driver you have to be absolutely certain you aren't being tailed. He'll know what to do."

Della Street merely nodded.

"When you're absolutely certain that nobody's following you," Mason went on, "beat it down to the Union Terminal. Pick up Carol Burbank. Tell her not to ask any questions and don't give her *any* information. Take her to the Woodridge. We know the manager there. I'll have things all fixed up by the time you arrive. Register under your own name, and register Carol under her name, only use her initials. In other words, if her middle name is Annie, register her as C. A. Burbank.—That will sound like a businessman rather than a woman—get me?"

Again Della Street nodded.

"Get rooms with a connecting bath," Mason said. "Have twin beds in your room. After you've been moved in and the bellboy has left, move Carol's baggage into your room. Lock the bathroom door so you've locked off the adjoining room. Keep Carol in with you."

"For how long?"

"Until you hear from me. Get her out of circulation and keep her out of circulation."

Della Street walked over to the hat closet, took out her hat, adjusted it on her head, and pulled her coat off a hanger.

Paul Drake said, "I don't like this, Perry."

Mason snapped irritably, "Neither do I, damn it. If you could only get some woman who . . ."

"Have a heart, Perry. You can't just pick up women for a job now. I'm lucky to have any female operatives at all. . . ."

Della Street walked to the door, hesitated, "Okay?" she asked Perry Mason.

Mason waved her on her way. "Go to it, Della—and luck."

13

The taxi driver said, "Okay, ma'am, you can bet your bottom dollar there's no one following you now."

Della Street, seated on the jump-seat where she could look out through the rear window of the taxicab and at the same time keep an eye on the road in front, said, "I guess we're all right now."

"Where to?" the cab driver asked.

"Union Terminal."

The cab swung around the corner. The driver flashed Della Street a glance of unconcealed approval. "What's the trouble—husband?"

Della nodded.

"A man married to a girl like you," the cab driver announced with some feeling, "had ought to know how fortunate he is. If he starts acting up mean on you, someone had ought to punch his snozzle."

Della Street said, "Perhaps it's partly my fault."

"*Your* fault!" the driver exclaimed. "Where do you get that noise? A man driving hacks gets so he can size people up. Anybody that can't get along with you is just one of those things."

"Thank you," Della said demurely.

The cab driver moved slightly in the seat, squared his shoulders. "You just get right out and go about your business when you get to the station, ma'am. If there's anybody waiting there that says anything to you, *I'll* see that you aren't annoyed."

"Oh, it isn't that," Della said hastily. "It's all right now. I know that he won't be there. He won't have any idea where I'm going."

The cabby said, "Well, he didn't follow us, if that's what you mean."

"That's what I mean."

The driver laughed. "If any guy was trying to tag along behind us, he's in the hospital by this time. You know how it is, us fellows that are driving traffic all the time, we get so we know what we can do and what we can't do. And we know just how to go about doing what we can do. Shucks, you take some private guy that gets out in a car maybe once in a week, and maybe don't' drive traffic over ten or fifteen hours a month. Why say, he doesn't stand a chance."

"Yes, I suppose so," Della agreed.

The cab rolled smoothly along, the driver silent for a while, then as it rolled up to the Union Terminal, the driver said, "I'm giving you one of my cards, ma'am. If you have any more places to go where you don't want to be followed, just get in touch with me. You can usually find me around where you picked me up this afternoon. That's my stand."

"Thank you."

"And remember that no one's going to push you around any when I'm there."

"You're very kind."

Della Street paid him the meter fare, gave him a twenty-five cent tip and a smile.

The driver, a look of dreamy abstraction in his eyes, watched her through the entrance of the depot, and only snapped back to the realities of life and the traffic regulations when the horn of a car behind made raucous protest.

Della found Carol Burbank standing near the telephone

booth in the section of the terminal reserved for telephone and telegraph service.

"Hello," Carol said with a quick smile and an impulsively outstretched hand. "Mr. Mason telephoned that you'd be down and meet me here."

Della Street nodded. "He's given me some rather definite instructions," she said.

"So he told me."

"He thinks that it's very important that you do *exactly* what he says."

"Naturally," Carol said laughing, "if I paid an attorney to tell me what to do, I'd be foolish to disregard his advice."

"Where's your father?" Della asked.

Carol frowned. "I wish I knew. I've been trying to get him on the phone."

"Did he go to Skinner Hills Friday afternoon and talk with Frank Palermo?"

"*Friday* afternoon?"

"Yes."

"Of course not. Friday was the day of the political meeting at the Surf and Sun Motel. Don't you remember?"

Della Street said very definitely, "Well, you're to come with me—and you'll have to stay out of circulation for a while. Those are the boss's orders."

"Keeping me away from newspaper reporters?"

"I didn't ask him," Della Street said and smiled. "One doesn't, you know."

"Yes, I can understand Mr. Mason may be rather impatient if one interrupts his high-speed mental processes to ask why this is done and why that is done. All right, let's go."

"I think we'd better take a cab," Della said.

They started toward the taxi stand.

Carol Burbank said, " I think I'll put on my coat and gloves. That cold, west wind is blowing again this afternoon. It was so nice up until half an hour ago, too."

"I'll hold your purse," Della offered.

Carol Burbank slipped into her coat, opened her purse and pulled out a pair of gloves. As she did so, a slip of pasteboard fluttered from the purse to the floor.

Della glanced inquiringly at Carol Burbank and saw Carol's face was a complete blank. Evidently she had failed to notice that bit of pasteboard.

Della Street turned back. A smiling man who had rushed forward to play the gallant raised his hat and extended the printed pasteboard.

Della Street flashed him a smile.

Carol Burbank turned to regard Della Street curiously, and Della, moved by some impulse, pushed the claim check down into the pocket of her coat. Not until they had moved out through the patio to the cab stand, did Della slip the pasteboard out of her pocket and give it a quick inspection.

It was a claim check at the parcel claim stand at the depot.

Abruptly Della said, "Just a minute, Miss Burbank, I want to call the boss about something. Do you mind waiting for just a minute?"

"Not at all. I'll go back with you."

"Oh, don't bother to do that. I'll just skip along and . . ."

"No, no. I'll come along."

"There's nothing that you want to get here at the depot, is there?"

"No."

"No baggage or anything?"

"Heavens, no! I just came down here because it was a good place to telephone and one can always find a cab here. These days it isn't easy to pick up a cab just when you want one."

Della said, "Yes, I know how it is. I had to wait so long a few days ago that I missed my appointment at my hairdresser. If you'll just excuse me a moment, Miss Burbank."

Della Street popped into a telephone booth, leaving Carol Burbank standing outside.

She dialed the unlisted number of the phone on Mason's desk. She heard the receiver lifted and Mason's voice saying cautiously, "Hello, who is this?"

"Della."

"Hello, Della. You okay?"

"Yes."

"You weren't followed?"

"No."

"You sure?"

"Yes. Not a chance."

"You have Carol?"

"Yes."

"You at the hotel now?"

"No, at the terminal. Listen, Chief, she opened her purse to take out her gloves and dropped a claim check. It's on the parcel checking service here. She must have left that package, or whatever it is, within the last hour or two . . ."

"Where's that check now?"

"I have it."

"Does she know it?"

"No. She hasn't realized she's lost it yet."

"All right, you have an envelope in your purse?"

"Yes."

"Write my name on it. Put in the claim check. When you get to the hotel, leave the envelope at the desk. I'll pick it up, go get the parcel and see what's in it. Got that straight?"

"Yes."

"Okay. Take care of yourself."

"I will. Bye, Chief."

"Bye, Della."

Della hung up, then moved around on the stool so that her shoulder hid what she was doing. She slipped an envelope out of her purse and scribbled Mason's name and the office address on it, inserted the pasteboard under the flap.

She rejoined Carol, and the two girls retraced their steps to the taxi stand and moved forward as a vacant cab drew up to the curb.

"Where to?" the starter asked.

Della said, "We're both together. It's the Woodridge Hotel."

"Sorry, we're not putting two people in a cab any more, you'll have to double up with . . . Where to, Mister?"

A man's voice said, "I want to go to Eleventh and Figueroa."

"All right, get in," the starter said, and then instructed the driver, "Take the young ladies to the Woodridge Hotel, and the man to Eleventh and Figueroa, Jack. Any baggage?"

It seemed that none of them had baggage.

The man, from the first, seemed definitely interested in his fellow travelers. It was two blocks, however, before he said tentatively, "Cooled off rather suddenly, didn't it?"

Carol Burbank smiled. "Yes, it did. But after all, one can expect that this time of year. It's a little early for the warm weather to set in."

"There certainly is a shortage of taxicabs," the man observed.

"Yes, isn't there."

"Not that I object," he said with a smile, "when it gives me a break like this. You girls from San Francisco?"

Carol looked inquiringly at Della Street. Della Street gave the man a somewhat vague smile and said simply, "No. I've been there, though."

The man said, "I live there. Swell place. Have to come down here once in a while on business. Always anxious to get back. This place is just a mass of people. San Francisco is a city."

"Watch out," Carol Burbank warned, "they shoot people for saying things like that down here."

"I can't help it. I think San Francisco . . . Say, you girls don't live here in Los Angeles, do you?"

Once more Carol looked to Della Street for guidance.

Della laughed. "What's the matter, are you afraid to voice your opinion if we do?"

"Well, of course—I don't want to seem discourteous."

"Oh, I'm certain the residents of Los Angeles get accustomed to hearing people from San Francisco refer to Los Angeles in terms of disparagement. But don't they have more sunshine here than they do in San Francisco? Don't you have lots of fog?"

"Fog!" the man exclaimed. "Why that's the thing that *makes* San Francisco. When that fog comes rolling in from the ocean, it peps you up. It's bracing, stimulating. There's a lot of rush and bustle in connection with San Francisco. Down here, people seem to have the hookworm. You girls really don't live here, do you?"

"What makes you think we don't?" Della said.

"Too much class—too much pep."

"I thought Hollywood was noted for its beautiful women."

"Oh, I guess it is, but they're synthetic. You girls are metropolitan, you don't act the way they do down here. You don't wear your clothes that way. You have something about you—something . . ."

"An air of urban sophistication," Carol Burbank finished.

The man said with some enthusiasm, "That's it exactly."

The girls laughed and, after a moment, the man joined them somewhat half-heartedly. "*I'm* kidding on the square," he protested. "You're stringing me along."

The cab drew up in front of the Woodridge Hotel.

The man said somewhat ruefully, "I'm sorry your hotel wasn't nearer Eleventh and Figueroa. Well, good-by."

They smiled at him, paid the cab driver and Della Street led the way into the hotel.

"Good afternoon," the clerk said and spun the rack containing the registration card around toward Della Street.

Della picked up the fountain pen, said in a low voice, "I'm from Mr. Mason's office. I . . ."

"Oh yes. I have reservations all made. You're Miss Street?"

"Yes."

Della registered, said to Carol Burbank, "I'll register for you. By the way, what's your middle name?"

"Edith, but I seldom use it."

"That's all right," Della said, and wrote the name C. E. Burbank on the register.

The clerk smacked his palm down on the call bell and called, "Front!"

Della Street slipped the addressed envelope out of her purse, placed it on the counter. "A message for Mr. Mason," she said. "He may pick it up a little later. Will you . . ."

"I'll be glad to see that he gets it. Will he call personally, or do you expect him to send a messenger? We . . ."

A man who had just entered the lobby walked rapidly toward the desk, cleared his throat importantly.

The clerk broke off to glance over Della Street's shoulder, said, "Just a moment, I'm busy with these two young ladies. Boy, will you take these ladies to six-twenty-four and six-twenty-six? Open the communicating bath and . . ."

"Just a minute," the man said.

Della Street didn't like the tone of his voice. She turned apprehensively as a big hand pulled back the lapel of a coat. She saw a gold shield incrusted with a number, insignia and lettering. The affable stranger who had been so enthusiastic over the charms of San Francisco was neither affable nor friendly now. He pushed Della slightly to one side, and his big hand clamped down on the envelope the clerk was still holding in open-mouthed amazement.

Della Street said angrily, "Will you kindly explain the meaning of this?"

His eyes were steely, hard and watchful. He said in a tone that rasped with offensive authority, "You two girls have an appointment at Headquarters. The same cab you came in is waiting outside." He turned to a plain-clothes man who had come up behind him. "Keep an eye on them, Mac, while I see what's in this envelope."

Mac moved close while the first officer pulled out the claim check. He gave the other a quick look at it, holding it in such a way that Carol Burbank couldn't see what it was.

"Okay, Mac, I'll get it. You take the girls to Headquarters. We'll meet there."

Carol Burbank said quite firmly, "I guess perhaps you people don't know who I am. You just can't do this to me."

The man who had been so genial a few minutes before regarded her with unsmiling authority. "Don't kid yourself we don't know who you are, Miss Burbank. It's because we know who you are that we're doing this. Come on, get in the cab. Or do you want to ride in the wagon?" he asked as Carol held back.

"I want to call my lawyer," Della Street announced with dignity.

"Sure, sure," the man said soothingly, "but you can't do it here. You don't want the whole hotel to know your business, do you? Come on. There's a phone at Headquarters. You'll have all the time in the world to call him when you get there."

"I want to call him from here," Della said, starting toward the phone booths, "and I don't care whether the whole world knows my business."

110

The officer's hand grasped her arm. He jerked her back, spun her around. "All right, if you have to do it the hard way," he said. "This is a pinch."

■

14

The room at Police Headquarters had barred windows, held a clean, somewhat battered table, nearly a dozen chairs, three huge brass cuspidors on rubber mats, and nothing else. It was a plain room, obviously designed for just one purpose. It was devoid of ornament and cheer. People who were held in that room were like cattle herded into the killing pen of a stockyard. They simply waited until such time as the persons who controlled their destinies were ready to receive them.

Della Street and Carol Burbank sat over on the far side of the table near the window. Across the table from them, and between them and the door, the police officer who had been delegated to "keep an eye" on them, rested an elbow on the table, propped his feet on the rung of an adjacent chair, and gave the girls a view of the somewhat beefy profile of a man slightly past middle age.

The passing of years had made him indifferent to feminine beauty, and long association with the police had utterly calloused him to human misery. His manner indicated that he had detached himself from the scene of which he was a part. His body hulked between the prisoners and the door, which constituted a discharge of his duty. His mind was far away, occupied with the mathematical percentages of his prospects for winning on the races the next afternoon; daydreaming what he would do when he became eligible for pension; and rehashing in his mind an argument he had had with his wife that morning, thinking somewhat ruefully of her natural aptitude for delivering an extemporaneous tongue lashing, whereas he hadn't thought of his best retorts until long afterward. His wife had a gift that way. No, damn it, she'd inherited it from her mother—that must be it. He remembered some of the scenes with his mother-in-law before she'd died some ten years ago. At that time, Mabel had been all worked up over the way the old lady used to have tantrums. That was before Mabel had got fat. She certainly had a good figure in those days. Well, come to think of it, he'd put on a little weight himself. Got pretty much out of shape after he quit that handball exercise. Thinking back on it, he couldn't remember exactly when it was he'd quit. It had been after a spell of the flu, and then they'd changed his hours for a while, and . . .

Della Street said firmly, "I insist upon the right to use the telephone."

The officer frowned at having his thoughts interrupted. He didn't even turn his eyes toward Della Street. He said mechanically, "If they book you, you'll have a right to call a lawyer."

"I demand that I be permitted to communicate with an attorney right now."

The officer didn't say anything. He was frowning, trying to think just what had happened to make him quit handball—it had had something to do with a police shake-up. He wondered if that was the time the captain had been facing a grand jury investigation over the squawk the woman had made who ran that house out on . . .

Della Street said firmly, "I insist upon my right to communicate with Mr. Perry Mason, who is both my employer and my attorney."

"That isn't getting you anywhere, sister."

"All right, you've heard me make the demand. We'll see whether it gets me anywhere or not. I think there's some law on the subject."

"You can talk to the Lieutenant."

"All right, let me talk to the Lieutenant."

"He'll see you when he's ready."

"Well, I'm ready now, and I'm not talking to the Lieutenant—I'm talking to you."

"I'm just following orders."

Della Street said, "You might find yourself on the spot, you know. Perry Mason isn't going to like this."

"Ma'am, the Lieutenant just don't give a damn whether Perry Mason likes it or whether he doesn't."

"And when he doesn't like a thing," Della Street went on, "he's very apt to do something about it. He might even prefer charges against you."

The officer's feet came down to the floor with a bang. He turned to look at Della Street now. "Charges against *me?*" he said.

"Exactly."

"On what grounds?"

"For refusing to let me communicate with a lawyer, for failing to take me before the nearest magistrate without unnecessary delay."

"Now wait a minute," the officer said. "You aren't arrested yet."

"Then why are you holding me here?"

"The D.A. wants to talk with you."

"I don't want to talk with the D.A."

"That's your hard luck."

"You mean I'm here as a witness?"

"Well, in a way—yes. There's a crime under investigation."

"If I'm held as a witness," Della Street said, "you have to get a court order to hold me. If I'm arrested, you have to take me before the nearest and most accessible magistrate without any unnecessary delay."

"Well, we're just sort of waiting to get the magistrate," the officer said with a smile.

"Have it your own way," Della said, "but when charges

114

are made against you, don't say I didn't warn you. You look like a man who has a long police career back of you. It would be a shame if you did something now that would keep you from getting a pension."

"Say, what are you talking about?"

"About the fact that if you are guilty of a violation of my rights, and if charges should be preferred against . . ."

"Say, listen, I'm just obeying orders."

"Orders that you're to hold me here without letting me communicate with a lawyer?"

"Well, that I'm to hold you here."

Della Street smiled triumphantly. "You know what the higher-ups will say when someone starts putting on the pressure. They'll say, 'Why, we just instructed that officer to give them seats in an anteroom. We didn't tell him they were under arrest. We supposed, of course, they were willing to remain there voluntarily in order to help us investigate the crime. We certainly didn't *tell* him they weren't to communicate with an attorney. We thought, of course, he'd know enough to see they weren't deprived of their constitutional rights. If he violated the law, he did it on his own. We aren't responsible. We never gave him any such orders.' "

The officer said, "Say, wait a minute. You're like my wife. Women are all the same."

He scraped back the chair and, frowning portentously, lumbered to the door. He opened it, stood in the corridor, holding the door in his hand so that it was open five or six inches.

Carol Burbank said, "Good work, Miss Street. You've got him worried."

The officer raised his voice, "P-s-s-s-s-t, Jim!"

Abruptly he pulled the door shut.

The girls were left alone for some five minutes, then the door opened again, and the officer said, "The Lieutenant will see you now."

"I have nothing to say to anyone."

"Well, you want to use a telephone, don't you?"

"Yes."

"Well, there isn't any telephone in this room. You want to go to a room where there's a telephone, or don't you?"

"Yes."

"All right, then come this way."

The girls arose, followed the officer down a corridor which echoed to the sound of their steps. The officer opened a door and, with a very evident gesture of relief, said, "Okay, Lieutenant, here they are."

Lieutenant Tragg sat at a plain oak desk in a corner of the room. There were three chairs arranged in a semicircle in front of the desk.

"Sit down," he invited courteously.

Della Street said, "I want to telephone Mr. Mason."

"I want to ask you a few questions first."

"I want to telephone Mr. Mason."

Tragg said, "Now, listen. I don't want to pick on you, Miss Street, but when Perry Mason starts using you to pull chestnuts out of the fire for him, I have no other alternative. I'm going to connect Perry Mason with what has happened, and the only way I can do it is through you."

"What's happened?" Della Street asked.

"You know as well as I do what's happened. You and Perry Mason have been trying to suppress evidence."

"Bosh!" Della said.

"You went whizzing down to pick up Miss Burbank and spirit her away where she couldn't be found."

"What are you talking about? I took Miss Burbank to a hotel and registered her under her own name. Does that look as though I were concealing a witness? All you had to do was consult the register and . . ."

"Yes, I know," Tragg said. "It was done very cleverly, but the purpose for which it was done was to conceal this witness."

116

"Try and prove it," Della challenged.

"That," Tragg said, "is the unfortunate part. Due to the clever ruse of registering Miss Burbank under her own name, I can't prove it."

"Then what are you holding me for?"

"But," Tragg added with a triumphant smile, "I can hold you on one thing—and that is your attempt to conceal evidence."

"What evidence?" Della Street asked.

With a sudden dramatic gesture, Lieutenant Tragg whipped open a drawer in his desk, pulled out a pair of woman's shoes. "I suppose," he said, "you'll say that you've never seen *these* before?"

"I haven't," Della Street promptly declared.

Tragg's smile was supercilious, "Unfortunately, Miss Street, that story doesn't check with the facts. Perry Mason instructed Miss Carol Burbank to take these shoes, wrap them in a brown paper parcel, take them to the parcel checking station at the Union Terminal, check them and get a receipt. She did that. She got a claim check. She passed the claim check on to you. You took the claim check, placed it in an envelope and wrote the name 'Perry Mason' on that envelope in your own handwriting."

For a long four or five seconds, Della Street said nothing. Then she asked, "What's wrong with those shoes?"

Lieutenant Tragg picked up a magnifying glass, examined a section of the shoe just above the leather sole. "There's nothing *wrong* with them, Miss Street. The shoes are all right. It's you who are in the wrong. Those shoes . . ."

The door abruptly jerked open, Perry Mason pushed his way into the room, "Okay, Lieutenant, that will be about all."

An officer showed his head through the door, "Did you send for him?" he asked.

"I did not," Lieutenant Tragg said.

The officer entered the room. "Out!" he said to Perry Mason.

Della Street said very rapidly, "Lieutenant Tragg, this is my attorney. If I am to be accused of any crime, he is my counsel. If I'm not to be accused of any crime, I have absolutely nothing to say as a witness, and will have nothing to say unless I am subpoenaed and examined in the regular manner."

Mason said, "As attorney for both of these young women, I demand that they be taken before the nearest and most accessible magistrate immediately."

Tragg's smile was dry. "Unfortunately, Mason, this is Sunday. I'm afraid you won't find any magistrate available until Monday morning when . . ."

"Don't kid yourself," Mason interrupted. "Judge Roxmann has done me the favor of going to his court. He's sitting there waiting."

Tragg slowly pushed back his chair. He sighed wearily. "All right," he surrendered, "that does it."

Mason motioned to Della and Carol.

"You mean we can go now?" Carol asked.

Tragg didn't answer. Mason moved over, held the door open. Della Street stalked out. Carol followed. Tragg said as Mason started to close the door, "She'll be back before midnight, Mason, and the next time she'll stay."

Mason pulled the door closed behind him. So far as giving any sign, he might not have heard what Tragg said.

15

Carol Burbank seated herself in Mason's office, said, "I heard what Lieutenant Tragg told you as we were leaving the office. How long have I got?"

"I don't know," Mason said. "It depends upon whether your father has been arrested, and on what he's said."

She said, "I don't think they can trap Father, only . . ."

"Only what?" Mason asked as her voice trailed off into silence.

She said, "He's on a spot."

"Tell me something I don't know—start talking—try telling the truth for a change."

"I'm afraid to."

"Damn it," Mason said, "I'm your lawyer. Whatever you say to me is confidential."

"If I tell you you'll quit representing us."

"Don't be silly," Mason snapped. "I *can't* quit. We've dragged Della into it. I've got to see *her* through. Give me the whole business right from the beginning."

Carol said, "Mr. Mason, this is going to sound terrible. Please don't judge me until I've finished."

Mason made an impatient gesture.

Carol said, "It goes back to something that happened years ago, something that has followed my father all through his life. Daphne Milfield knew about it and used that knowledge to make Father back her husband in this Skinner Hills project."

"Blackmail?" Mason asked.

"Not that crude, but . . . Well, yes, if you want to call it that."

"I think," Mason told her, "I'm going to want to call it that."

Carol said, "It was all done very nicely. Daphne Milfield rang Father up—just wanted to renew an old friendship. She would, of course, respect his secret. He could trust her discretion absolutely. A week or two later Fred Milfield called on Father. He had this Skinner Hills deal that he wanted financed. It meant so much to him and Daphne was so anxious to have it go through."

"What happened?"

"Well, of course, on a deal of that kind, you can't take any chances on having your plans get out before you have everything under control. Fred Milfield knew all about how to go about it, and he made his own arrangements with a man named Van Nuys whom I have never met. These two pretended they were interested in Karakul sheep and started buying up all the property. The field was even better than anyone had dared anticipate. Father pretended he was putting down a deep water well on one of the properties. They struck the oil bearing sand even before they were ready."

"Then Milfield and Van Nuys are rich?"

"They would have become rich in time. That was the trouble. There is one thing Father simply won't stand for and that is any double-crossing. He found out that Fred Milfield had been knocking down on him."

"How?" Mason asked.

"The idea was to have all the papers made out for only a fair consideration," Carol explained. "But there could be cash payments made on the side when the deals were difficult to close otherwise. Fred started lying about that. He'd make a payment of one thousand and then tell Dad it was five thousand. Since it was all handled off the record and in the form of cash, there was no way of checking on him."

"How did your father find out?"

"He became suspicious. So Friday afternoon he went to call on Frank Palermo. He pretended to be another speculator. He picked Palermo because he knew that having signed one contract wouldn't stop Palermo from signing another one."

"What did he find out?"

"That Palermo had only been paid one thousand dollars."

"How much did Milfield claim he'd paid Palermo?"

"Four thousand."

"Then what?"

"Father was terribly angry. He tried to get in touch with Milfield, then left word for Milfield to telephone him at the yacht club. Father was angry about that accident, too. Milfield had been moving Karakul sheep in some trucks that were registered in Father's name. There'd been an accident and the man that was in it had got the license number of the truck and Milfield hadn't done anything about it. Father instructed his lawyers to make a settlement no matter what it cost. He was afraid that some shrewd lawyer would—well, do just what you did, investigate the license number, find out what was going on under cover, and start skyrocketing the price of some of the property on which deals hadn't been closed."

Mason said, "Let's get back to Milfield and your father. What happened?"

"Milfield got Father on the phone late Friday morning. Father told him just what he'd discovered. You see, Father could have terminated Milfield's connection with any future profit if he could prove fraud and embezzlement, and Milfield was in a panic."

"What did he say?"

"He said that he would bring Palermo down to the yacht and make him admit he was lying. Of course that

121

didn't fool Father any. Father knew Palermo could be bribed to say anything."

"And Milfield went down to the yacht?" Mason asked.

"Yes. He didn't get there until late afternoon, however."

"What happened?"

"Milfield tried to bluster and threaten and took a punch at Father and Father knocked him down, climbed up the companionway, turned Milfield's rowboat loose, got into the dinghy, started the outboard and took the dinghy ashore. He was intending to have Milfield arrested."

"Why didn't he?"

"He got in touch with me. I jumped in my car and beat it down to the yacht club. I persuaded Father not to call the police until we knew what sort of shape Milfield was in. The dinghy was tied at the float. I got aboard and dashed out to the yacht."

"What did you find?"

"Milfield was lying on the floor—dead. He'd evidently hit his head against the threshold of the stateroom when he was knocked down."

"Why didn't you notify the police?"

"I couldn't—because of that thing in Father's past."

"What was it?"

"He'd had a fight with a man several years ago in New Orleans. The man fell against an andiron and was killed. There were no witnesses. Father got out of it all right, but now if the police found out about his past record, they'd say that *both* cases had been deliberate murder; that Father had knocked the man unconscious and then deliberately cracked his head against the andiron, and had done the same thing in *this* case."

Mason began pacing the floor.

Carol said, "You know the rest of it. I went back and told Father Milfield was dead. Father almost killed himself that night. Then I worked out this scheme of giving him an alibi. I knew that Lassing and a party were at the

Surf and Sun Motel. He'd telephoned late Friday night and again Saturday morning trying to get in touch with Father. So I had Judson Beltin rush me up to the Surf and Sun Motel. We tried to catch Lassing before he'd checked out, but Lassing had gone."

"So what did you do?"

"So Beltin paid the rent for another day on the apartment, pretending that he was one of Lassing's party."

"And then you planted the stuff?"

"Yes."

"Where was your father?"

"He was keeping under cover at the restaurant where we found him."

"How did the police know he was there?"

She said, "At an hour which had been very carefully arranged between us, Judson Beltin rang up the police and gave them an anonymous tip. I wanted the police to find him there and then for us to come in at just the right psychological moment and have Father pull the key out of his pocket—well, you know how it happened."

Mason said, "You *almost* made it stick."

"I know."

"Did you," Mason asked, "try to tamper with Lassing?"

"Yes. That's where I made my big mistake. I rang Lassing up and told him as a favor to me to refuse to answer any questions about the people who were with him; to pretend that they were big-shots and if anybody asked if Father had been there to—well, he wasn't to tell any lies, but was simply to refuse to answer questions in such a way that it would seem that Father and some business associates had been there and Lassing was simply not giving out the information."

Mason said, "All right, let's get back to what happened at the yacht. How soon after his trouble with Milfield did *you* get there?"

"It was an hour or so. I was at a cocktail party."

"Where was your father?"

"He stayed at the office."

"What time was it when you got to the yacht club?"

"I don't know. It was still daylight, I remember that."

"You jumped in the dinghy and started the outboard motor and went out to the yacht?"

"Yes."

"And found Milfield's body?"

"Yes."

"Where was it lying?"

"Stretched out on the floor. The head was within just an inch or two of that brass-covered threshold."

"The body wasn't there when the police found it."

"I know, the boat tilted when the tide went out and the body rolled over to the starboard side of the cabin."

"How about that bloody footprint?"

"I didn't know I'd stepped in the blood until I'd started up the stairs. Then the minute I put my right foot on the tread I felt that peculiar sticky feeling and looked down and saw what had happened."

"What did you do?"

"I took my shoe off—both shoes, climbed up the companionway in my stocking feet."

"Then what?"

"After I got in the dinghy I washed my shoes off. I thought I'd got rid of all the blood. It wasn't until afterwards that I realized that I hadn't. Some of it had dried between the upper part and the sole. I didn't know how to get rid of them. So I simply decided to wrap them in a parcel, take them down to the parcel checking counter at the Union Terminal and leave them."

"And the boat was on an even keel and the body of Fred Milfield hadn't been moved when you got aboard?"

"That's right. It was lying right there, the head almost touching the threshold."

Mason said, "There *has* to be a way out of this mess. Not on your account. Not on your father's account, but on Della's account."

124

He continued pacing the floor. Carol watched him silently.

Abruptly Mason whirled, picked up the phone. "They weren't following Della Street," he said. "That means they were following you. They'd followed every move you made. There must have been more than one detective. This claim check fell out of your purse. Someone picked it up and handed it to Della. Did you see him do it?"

"I remember seeing a man hand her something."

"What did he look like?"

"He was around fifty and wore a gray suit. He had a very agreeable smile and . . ."

"Forget that agreeable smile. That was come-on. What color were his eyes, what color was his hair?"

Carol shook her head dubiously and said, "There was something funny about his nose. It seemed—it seemed rather broad."

"Broken?"

"It could have been. Yes, that could have been it."

"How tall?"

"Medium height."

"Heavy?"

"Well, broad-shouldered."

Mason dialed Paul Drake's number on the telephone. "Paul," he said, "I want all the dope on any police detectives who might be connected with homicide. I want to find out something about a man who may have been a prize fighter in his earlier days, about fifty, broken nose, broad-shouldered, medium height, light complexion, gray suit. Drop everything else and get the dope on him."

"What's so important about him?" Drake asked.

"He's the one who handed Della Street the claim check after Carol dropped it. I've got to try to show that he was a police detective and that the police themselves pushed this claim check into Della's hand. Make a police frame-up out of it. Get me?"

"I get you," Drake said dubiously, "but that isn't going to be easy. If you . . ."

Peremptory knuckles banged on the door of Mason's private office.

Mason quietly dropped the receiver back into place, walked across the office and pulled the door open.

Lieutenant Tragg and two uniformed officers were standing in the hallway. Tragg's smile was quietly confident.

"I told you I'd be back for her, Mason," he said. "And this time it won't do you any good to have a magistrate waiting. We're ready to make a charge now."

Mason turned to Carol Burbank. "Okay, sister," he said grimly, "this is it."

She said to Mason, "Please find Father and . . ."

"Don't be silly," Mason said. "The reason Tragg is ready to put a charge against you now is that he's . . ."

"Got your father," Tragg interrupted to finish.

"Exactly," Mason said.

16

■

Judge Newark presided at the preliminary hearing of Roger Burbank and Carol Burbank, and the crowded courtroom gave evidence that the public realized only too well the underlying significance and far reaching importance of this hearing.

Giving some indication of the importance which the district attorney's office attached to the case, was the fact that Hamilton Burger, the district attorney, was present in person, assisted by Maurice Linton, one of the most able of the younger trial deputies.

Maurice Linton, a slim, fiery man with quick, nervous gestures and a gift for oratory, arose to make a brief opening statement.

"Your Honor," he said, "while I realize that it is somewhat unusual to make an opening statement in a preliminary hearing of this nature, yet, inasmuch as much of our evidence will be circumstantial, and as it seems quite evident from the number of witnesses subpoenaed and the preparations made by the defense that an attempt will be made to throw this case out of court at the end of this hearing, I want the court to understand what we are trying to prove.

"We intend to prove that Roger Burbank had a violent altercation with the deceased on the night of the murder; that thereafter, the defendant, Carol Burbank, endeavored to give her father a false alibi by suborning perjury. We intend to show that at an auto court where a political meeting was claimed to have been held, a collection of empty bottles holds the fingerprints of Carol Burbank, of Judson Beltin, and of no one else. We will also prove that the defendant, Roger Burbank, a strong, powerful man, a trained boxer in his youth, inveigled the decedent to his yacht and there murdered him."

The judge looked to Perry Mason, "Do you desire to make any statement, Mr. Mason?"

Jackson, seated at Mason's left, leaned forward and whispered, "I think he's impressed by that statement. You'd better say something."

Mason merely shook his head. "We'll wait until we see how the case develops, Your Honor."

"Very well. The prosecution will call its first witness."

The prosecution called Lieutenant Tragg, introduced evidence of the finding of the body of Fred Milfield, the identification of the body, the position in which the body was found, the place where the yacht was moored, virtually all of the elements necessary to establish a *corpus delicti.*

"You may cross-examine," Linton announced.

Mason seemed elaborately casual in his cross-examination. "The murder was committed aboard a yacht?"

"Yes."

"And where was the yacht anchored?"

"I think if counsel will wait a little while," Burger said, "that question will be satisfactorily answered. We have some witnesses who will produce charts, photographs and maps."

"Then," Mason said, "I feel that I should be entitled to postpone my cross-examination of this witness until after those are introduced."

"No objection," Burger said.

Mason announced with a smile, "That's all, Lieutenant."

Burger next called a surveyor, introduced a chart of the

estuary, showing the place where the yacht was anchored, showing diagrams of the interior of the yacht, a diagram of the deck, of the cabin, then announced triumphantly, "You may cross-examine."

Mason said, "The yacht was anchored at the place you have marked with a cross on People's Exhibit Number One. Is that correct?"

"That's correct."

"How deep was the water at that point?"

The surveyor smiled, "I don't know. I located the yacht by triangulation, and superimposed the location upon a chart of the estuary."

"Very interesting. And you don't know how deep the water was?"

"No, I'm a surveyor—not a diver."

The courtroom laughed.

Mason didn't even smile. He said, "That's all."

The surveyor was followed by a photographer who introduced various photographs showing the interior of the cabin, the body of Fred Milfield sprawled on the floor, the yacht riding at anchor, a view of the starboard side of the yacht; then a view of the port side of the yacht; then one of the bow, and one of the stern.

"Cross-examine," Linton said.

Mason said very quietly, "How deep was the water at that point?"

A titter ran through the courtroom.

The photographer said quickly, "I don't know. I'm a photographer, not a diver."

The titter swelled into audible merriment. The judge rapped for order.

Mason said casually, "That's all."

Jackson, somewhat concerned, leaned forward to whisper to Mason, "I think the audience in the courtroom is laughing at you."

"Do you, indeed," Mason whispered without even bothering to turn around.

Burger called Mrs. Daphne Milfield.

Mrs. Milfield, attired in black, her eyes still slightly swollen from weeping, took the witness stand.

"You are the widow of Fred Milfield, the decedent?" the district attorney asked with that sympathetic consideration which district attorneys always show for the widows in murder cases.

"Yes," she answered in a voice that was hardly audible.

"Mrs. Milfield, are you acquainted with Roger Burbank, one of the defendants in this case?"

"Yes."

"How long have you known him?"

"Ten years."

"Do you know whether Roger Burbank asked your husband to meet him at any designated place on the day your husband met his death?"

"Yes. Mr. Burbank telephoned."

"When?"

"About eleven-thirty that morning."

"Who answered the telephone?"

"I did."

"And did you recognize the voice of Roger Burbank?"

"I did."

"The voice which you have known for some ten years?"

"Yes."

"And what did Mr. Burbank say?"

"When he found Fred wasn't there, he said he was very anxious to get in touch with him, that he wanted Fred to come aboard his yacht for a conference at five o'clock that afternoon. He said his yacht would be at the usual place, that the thing he wanted to see Fred about was a matter of greatest importance."

"And you're certain this was Roger Burbank with whom you were talking?"

"Yes."

"Did you communicate this message to your husband?"

"I did."

"When?"

"About twenty minutes after the call was received."

"How?"

"My husband called up on the telephone to tell me he wouldn't be home for dinner, might not get in until after midnight."

"And you gave him this message from Roger Burbank?"

"Yes."

"What did your husband say, if anything?"

"He said he had already talked over the telephone with Mr. Bur . . ."

"Objected to," Mason interposed, "as incompetent, irrelevant and immaterial, not part of the *res gestae*, and therefore hearsay."

"Sustained," Judge Newark ruled.

"You may cross-examine," Hamilton Burger announced.

Jackson leaned forward to whisper to Mason, "That 'knowing him for ten years' business is a trap. He's hoping you'll walk into it and give her an excuse to get that old case in front of the court."

Mason nodded, said to the witness, "You say you have known Roger Burbank for ten years, Mrs. Milfield?"

"Yes," she answered in a voice that was hardly more than a whisper.

"Have you known him well?"

"Quite well."

"Was he in Los Angeles all of that time?"

"No."

"Where was he when you first got acquainted with him?"

"In New Orleans. I did some yachting, and Mr. Burbank was an enthusiastic yachtsman. We met that way. Actually, the first time I met him I was rowing a skiff out to a yacht, and Mr. Burbank in another rowboat started racing me."

"You have known him longer than your husband?"

"Yes."

"Was it through you that your husband got in touch with Mr. Burbank?"

"I believe so, yes."

"There was an interval of some years during which you hadn't seen Mr. Burbank?"

"Yes."

"And then you telephoned him?"

"I did."

"You mentioned your old acquaintanceship?"

"Yes."

A look of triumphant satisfaction began to manifest itself upon the district attorney's face.

"Just what did you say to him, Mrs. Milfield?"

She flashed a glance at the district attorney, received in return what might have been a signal, said very rapidly, "I took pains to assure him that I would say nothing about the trouble he had been in in New Orleans when he had killed a man with a blow of his fist."

The judge frowned.

Mason, not changing his voice in the least, said, "But, notwithstanding that promise, you did tell your husband?"

"Well, I'd already told Fred."

"And did you tell any of your husband's business associates—Harry Van Nuys, for instance?"

"Yes, I told him."

"Anyone else?"

"No, just these two."

"And told them so they could go to Burbank and force him to finance them . . ."

"Absolutely not!"

"Then why did you tell them?"

"Just because I thought my husband had a right to know."

"And how about Van Nuys? Did you think he had a right to know?"

"Of course," Burger objected, "this inquiry is now going far afield, Your Honor."

Mason said, "Not at all, if the Court please. The Court will have noticed the eager alacrity with which the witness rushed into the discussion of Burbank's past. I am now showing bias, as well as asking her to elaborate on the answer she was so anxious to rush into the record."

"It is only natural this witness *should* have a bias," Burger snapped. "After all, this man murdered her husband."

"And it is only fair that I have a chance to show the extent of that bias," Mason said.

"Answer the question," the judge instructed. "The question was whether you thought a certain Harry Van Nuys had a right to know about this former trouble Burbank had been in."

"Well, he was my husband's business associate."

"And, therefore, entitled to know?" Mason asked.

"In a way, yes."

"Because you considered the information a business asset?"

"No! Absolutely not."

"But the information was used as a business asset, was it not?"

"By whom?"

"By your husband and Harry Van Nuys."

"That calls for hearsay," Burger objected. "This witness wouldn't know about anything that took place between her husband and Burbank except through what her husband may have told her. Moreover it calls for a conversation between husband and wife."

"The question was whether she knew," the court said. "That calls for her own knowledge."

"I don't know—of my knowledge," Mrs. Milfield said sweetly.

"But prior to this conversation you had with Burbank your husband had never met him?"

133

"No."

"Nor Harry Van Nuys?"

"No."

"But within a week or ten days after you told them of Burbank's past they *had* met him and *had* arranged with Burbank to finance them in an extensive business venture?"

"I don't think Mr. Van Nuys ever met Burbank."

"Your husband handled all the business of getting the financing?"

"Yes."

"Therefore Van Nuys had no reason to meet Mr. Burbank?"

"Well—no."

"Therefore, the only reason your husband went to see Burbank was to get money?"

"Backing."

"Financial backing?"

"Yes."

"In the form of cash?"

"Yes."

"Now then," Mason said, pointing his finger at the witness, "did you remonstrate with your husband for taking advantage of a situation which you had disclosed to him, for blackmailing Roger Burbank into advancing him money, and . . ."

"Your Honor," Burger objected, jumping to his feet, "this is incompetent, irrelevant and immaterial. Moreover, it calls for a privileged communication between husband and wife, it is far afield from any questions covered in the direct examination and I object to it specifically on the ground that it is not proper cross-examination."

"The objection is sustained on the privileged communication point," the judge ruled.

Mason said, "Now then, Mrs. Milfield, I'll direct your attention to the Saturday when the body was discovered.

You were in your apartment at that time, and I called on you there, did I not?"

"Yes."

"You'd been crying?"

"Objected to as improper cross-examination," the district attorney said.

"It may show bias," Mason pointed out to the court.

"Overruled."

"I called on you there?" Mason asked.

"Yes."

"And you had been crying?"

"Yes."

"And while I was there, Lieutenant Tragg of the Homicide Squad arrived, did he not?"

"Yes."

"And I told you that Lieutenant Tragg was connected with the Homicide Squad and asked you if you knew anyone who had been murdered and you said, 'It may have been my . . .' and then stopped. Did you not so state?"

"Yes"

"And you had in mind that it was your husband?"

"Yes."

"What made you think it was your husband, Mrs. Milfield?"

"Because—because he hadn't been home all night, and because I knew he'd had trouble with Roger Burbank; and that Mr. Burbank had claimed my husband had been guilty of falsifying his accounts."

"That's all," Mason said.

Burger's re-direct examination was triumphant. "And," he announced to the witness, "Mr. Mason, championing your cause just because Lieutenant Tragg happened to be downstairs, advised you to start peeling onions so that it would account for the tear-swollen appearance of your eyes, didn't he?"

Mason said, "Certainly, I did."

"Answer the question," Burger told the witness.

"Yes."

"Now *why* did Mr. Mason do that?"

The judge looked down at Mason and said, "I think this is objectionable, Mr. Mason, as not being proper re-direct examination and calling for a conclusion of the witness—in case you care to object to it."

"I don't care to object to it," Mason said. "I am quite willing to have it appear that I gave this young woman some gratuitous advice which would enable her to . . ."

"To save her face," Burger sneered.

Mason smiled and said, "Not to save her face, Counselor, merely to account for its appearance."

The courtroom burst into laughter.

The judge, smiling himself, pounded the courtroom into silence with his gavel. "Any further re-direct?" he asked.

"None, Your Honor."

"Re-cross?"

"None," Mason said.

"The witness is excused. Call your next witness, Mr. Burger."

Burger said grimly, "Your Honor, I am going to call my next witness slightly out of order, but I think I can show a pattern which I can presently connect up with other evidence, if the Court will bear with me."

"Very well."

"J. C. Lassing," Burger called.

Mr. Lassing, a stoop-shouldered man in the late fifties, with a dejected appearance, took the witness stand and painfully avoided meeting the eyes of either of the defendants.

"Your name is J. C. Lassing. You are an oil-drilling contractor, and you reside at sixty-eight forty-two La Brea Avenue, Colton, California?" Burger asked.

"Yes."

"Now then, on the Saturday in question, when the

body of Fred Milfield was discovered, you were in or near Santa Barbara, were you not?"

"Yes."

"On the Friday night previous, you had occupied cottages Thirteen and Fourteen at the Surf and Sun Motel on the coast highway between Los Angeles and San Francisco?"

"Yes."

"That is a short distance below Santa Barbara—between Ventura and Santa Barbara?"

"Yes." .

"And did you have any communication with anyone while you were there?"

"Yes."

"A telephone communication?"

"Yes."

"With whom?"

"Objected to," Mason said, "incompetent, irrelevant and immaterial."

"Sustained."

"Was it with one of these defendants?"

"Yes."

"Then I will ask you what this conversation was."

"Same objection," Mason said.

The judge frowned. "If it appears this conversation was with one of the defendants, Mr. Mason . . ."

Mason said, "If the Court please, it's perfectly proper for Counsel to ask this witness if he recognized the voices of either of the defendants, and if either of the defendants made any admissions to him over the telephone. But as to anything this witness may have said to the defendants, it's entirely incompetent, irrelevant and immaterial."

"I think that's right," the judge ruled.

"But Your Honor," Burger protested, "I want to connect this up. I want to show that because of the conversation, the defendants knew where this witness was staying, knew that he was at the Surf and Sun Motel."

"What's that got to do with it?" the judge asked.

"I'll connect that up with my next witness."

"Well," the judge said somewhat hesitantly, "I'm going to admit it if you change your question so that it covers only that specific point."

"Very well, Your Honor," Mr. Burger said. "Mr. Lassing, I will ask you if you communicated with the defendant, or with his office and told him where you were staying?"

"Well, I communicated with his office."

"With whom did you talk?"

"With Mr. Judson Beltin."

"And who is Mr. Beltin?"

"He is the secretary of Roger Burbank—sort of a manager."

"You know that, do you?"

"Yes."

"Of your own knowledge?"

"Yes."

"You've had business dealings with Mr. Burbank through Mr. Beltin?"

"Yes."

"And what did you tell Mr. Beltin?"

"I asked Mr. Beltin if I could get those drilling contracts on the Skinner Hills property. I told him I was there at the Surf and Sun Motel and I was going to be there until noon and asked him to get in touch with me if he had any definite answer to give me. He told me that . . ."

"I really see nothing to be gained by introducing the conversation of Mr. Beltin," the judge ruled. "I presume, Mr. District Attorney, it is your contention that Mr. Beltin subsequently communicated this information to one or both of the defendants, and that has some bearing upon the case?"

"Yes, Your Honor."

"I will let the answer stand up to that point, but I don't think that any conversation between Beltin and this witness is at all pertinent."

"Very well, Your Honor. I will now ask you, Mr. Lassing, what time you checked out of the Surf and Sun Motel?"

"Right around ten o'clock in the morning."

"When was this conversation you had with Mr. Judson Beltin?"

"Late Friday afternoon, about four forty-five, and also Saturday."

"There were some people occupying the two cottages with you?"

"Yes."

"Who were they?"

"Some of my associates—a driller and a geologist of my own, a man who gives me some financial backing at times, and another man who has an interest in my business."

"You had been investigating the Skinner Hills oil field?"

"Yes."

"How did you know that it was an oil field?"

"Well," Lassing said, scratching his head, "I did know it, and I didn't. I just happened to stumble onto it. I saw that Milfield and Burbank were getting together and buying up a lot of property. Well, us oil men sort of keep an eye on any large-scale movements in potential oil properties. They'd organized a Karakul Fur Company, but that didn't fool me any."

"So you went out and looked the ground over?" Burger asked.

"Yes."

Burger said, "Now then, Mr. Lassing, I'm going to ask you a question. Did you have any conversation with one of the defendants concerning your occupancy of the Surf and Sun Motel some time after you had checked out?"

Lassing fidgeted, then said, "Yes."

"With whom?"

"Carol Burbank."

"What did you say?"

"I take it," Judge Newark said, "the district attorney understands this question is not to call for extraneous matters, but only for some declaration which will have some bearing upon the case?"

"Yes, Your Honor."

"Answer the question."

"Well," Lassing said, "she asked me if I'd say that—well, if I'd just refuse to give the names of the people who occupied the cottages with me, just make it look as though I had something to conceal—just not give out any information about who they were."

"And what did you do?"

"Well, I told her all right, I'd do that."

"Is this," Mason asked somewhat scornfully, "the grounds upon which you're going to claim a subornation of perjury?"

"Yes," Burger snapped.

Mason smiled, "She didn't ask him to commit any perjury."

"I think she did," Burger said.

"Never mind the discussion between counsel," the judge ruled. "Go ahead with your examination, Mr. Burger."

"That's all."

"Any questions on cross-examination, Mr. Mason?"

Mason smiled, said, "Yes, Your Honor. Mr. Lassing, I will ask you if Carol Burbank, at any time, asked you to testify to anything that was false?"

"Well, no."

"Did she ask you to make any statements whatever that were false in character?"

"Well, she asked me to just keep quiet."

"Exactly. She asked you to keep quiet. She didn't ask

you not to make a true statement in the event you were called as a witness?"

"Well, no."

"But just to keep quiet, is that right?"

"Yes."

"Not to divulge the names of the persons who occupied those cabins with you?"

"That's right."

"She specifically asked you to say her father was not there, didn't she?"

"Why no."

"She asked you not to mention the names of any person as having been in that motel with you, didn't she? Or did I understand your testimony correctly?"

"That's right. Yes sir."

"And in your opinion any person would include her father?"

"Oh, I see what you're getting at now! Well, she asked me to refuse to tell the name of any person who was there—to act as secretive as I could about the whole business."

"Asked you to refuse to say her father was there?"

"To refuse to mention the name of anyone who was there."

"To refuse to say her father was there?"

"Well, if you want to put it that way—I was to refuse to give out *any* name—any name at all."

"To refuse to say her father was there?"

"Yes."

"That's all, Mr. Lassing. Thank you."

Mason smiled triumphantly, looked over at the prosecutor's table and said, "If that's suborning perjury, I'll eat it."

Lassing left the witness stand.

"It certainly shows an attempt on the part of the defendant, Carol Burbank, to give her father some sort of a fictitious alibi," the district attorney stormed.

141

"The witness didn't say she asked him to declare her father was present. You can't prove an alibi unless you swear someone *was* there. She asked him to refuse to say her father was there."

"Well, even so, she wanted *us* to assume that her father was present."

"Whatever one wants the district attorney's office to assume," Mason said, "is purely a personal and private matter. That's certainly a far cry from suborning perjury."

"I'm not going to bicker with Counsel," Burger lashed out. "I'll prove it before I'm done. I now want to recall Lieutenant Tragg to the stand. If the Court please, I used him only for the purpose of proving the *corpus delicti* in connection with the first part of his testimony."

"Very well," the court ruled.

Tragg returned to the witness stand.

"Did you," Burger asked, "have any conversation on Saturday, the day the body of Fred Milfield was discovered, with Carol Burbank?"

"Yes."

"Where did this conversation take place?"

"In a restaurant known, I believe, as the 'Dobe Hut,' between Los Angeles and Calabasas."

"And who was present at that conversation?"

"Mr. Roger Burbank, one of the defendants, and George Avon of the Los Angeles police."

"And what was said at that time?"

"The defendant, Carol Burbank, stated that her father had been attending a political conference; that under the circumstances he should no longer try to keep that conference a secret, but should tell us where he was and what transpired."

"Did she say that conference took place at the Surf and Sun Motel?"

"Well," Tragg said, "she implied it."

"Can you remember her exact language?"

"Unfortunately, I can't. I was more interested in Roger Burbank at the time."

"Did Roger Burbank make any statement with reference to that?"

"He put his hand down in his pocket and took out a key to Cabin Fourteen at the Surf and Sun Motel."

"And did he tell you he had stayed there?"

"Well, he certainly intimated that he had."

"That," Mason announced, "is a conclusion of the witness and should be stricken on that ground."

"I think so," the court ruled. "This witness is a police officer and he should be able to tell exactly what the defendant said."

"Well," Tragg said smiling, "he put his hand down into his pocket, took out a key to Cottage Fourteen at this motel, and handed that key to me."

"And did the defendant, Roger Burbank, thereafter accompany you to the Surf and Sun Motel and identify a razor of his which was found?"

"He did."

"And did Carol Burbank tell you that her father's razor was to be found in Cottage Fourteen of the Surf and Sun Motel?"

"She did."

"You may cross-examine," Burger said.

Mason's smile was suave. "Carol Burbank told you her father's razor was there?"

"Yes."

"Did she tell you that her father had been there?"

"Well, I can't remember that she said so, in so many words, but she inferred it."

"You mean that you inferred it from the fact that his razor was there?"

"Well, in a way, yes. If you're going to put it in just that way."

Mason smiled. "I want to put it in just that way. Now then, she told you that her father's razor was there."

"Yes."

"And did the defendant, Roger Burbank, tell you his razor was there?"

"Yes, subsequently."

"And pointed out the razor to you?"

"Yes."

"And identified it?"

"Yes."

"And *was* it his razor?"

Tragg seemed uncomfortable. "I don't know."

"Exactly," Mason said dryly. "He told you his razor was there. His daughter told you his razor was there. You found the razor there. You have taken no steps one way or another to prove whether or not it was his razor, have you?"

"It was planted."

"Never mind your deductions, Lieutenant. Have you taken any steps to show whether that was or was not the razor of the defendant, Roger Burbank?"

"Well, no. I assume it was his razor."

Mason smiled.

"So Carol Burbank told you her father's razor was at this motel. Roger Burbank admitted his razor might be there. You took him up there—and found his razor was there. Thereupon, you tried to browbeat him into admitting that he had been there—and he denied it, didn't he?"

"He denied it half-heartedly, so I'd think he was lying, and I *didn't* try to browbeat him."

"But he denied it?"

"Half-heartedly, yes."

"Half-heartedly, quarter-heartedly or three-quarter-heartedly, he denied it?"

"Yes."

"I submit, Your Honor," Mason said, "that the fraction, or percentage of the man's heart that was in his statement is the conclusion of a prejudiced witness. The *fact* is *what* the man said."

Judge Newark nodded. His eyes were twinkling. "Proceed, Mr. Mason. The Court is making due allowances."

Mason turned to Lieutenant Tragg. "And the defendant, Roger Burbank, told you that if you asked him publicly whether he had stayed at the Surf and Sun Motel the night before, he would have to deny it. Is that right?"

"Yes. But when he said that, I took it as an admission he was there."

"I see," Mason said. "That was merely your own interpretation of what he said?"

"It was the way I understood his words."

"Fortunately, Lieutenant, we are to judge the case by what he said, not by what you understood."

"His daughter, Carol, said he'd been there at the restaurant."

"Pardon me," Mason said, "I was present at that time. Didn't Carol merely suggest that a political conference might have been held at the Surf and Sun Motel the night before, and then didn't she tell her father that the time had come for him to speak up and tell you exactly where he had been, and not try to protect the political careers of a lot of Sacramento bigwigs; and didn't the defendant then reach in the pocket of his coat and take out a key and put it on the table, and didn't you forthwith grab that key and see that it was the key to Cottage Fourteen at the Surf and Sun Motel?"

"Well, yes."

"The defendant, Roger Burbank, didn't ever say in so many words that he had been there, did he?"

"Well, he produced that key."

"And then, after he had produced that key, he looked you straight in the eyes and told you that if you asked him if he had been present at the Surf and Sun Motel the night before he would deny it?"

"Well, I don't remember exactly how it happened."

"And didn't Carol Burbank say, 'But Dad, your razor is there on the shelf,' or words to that effect?"

"Well, yes."

"And you took that as an admission by Carol Burbank that her father had been there?"

"Well, his razor was there," Tragg blurted.

"Exactly," Mason said. "His razor was there. I take it that you will agree, Lieutenant, it's no crime for a man to put his razor any place he happens to choose?"

"Well, taken in connection with all the circumstances," Tragg said, "the inference is obvious."

"You may draw that inference if you want," Mason said, "but I think a jury will prefer to try the case on the facts. And if you're going to make any claim of perjury, you've got to prove a false *statement*, not that, as in this case, the person charged made a *true* statement in such a manner that the police in charge thought it was untrue. It's what a man actually *says* that counts, and to be perjury it must be under oath."

"The perjury is what they wanted Lassing to commit," Tragg said.

Mason raised his brows. "Oh, did someone ask him to swear to a falsehood?"

"We've been all over that," Tragg said.

"So we have!" Mason smiled. "Now, Lieutenant Tragg, you were called to the yacht of Roger Burbank on Saturday morning when the body was discovered?"

"Yes."

"And made some examination there?"

"Yes."

"And found the bloody imprint of a shoe on one of the treads of the companionway?"

"I'm coming to that," Burger interposed hastily, "with another witness."

"I'm coming to it now," Mason said. "In fact, I'm already at it. Can you answer that question, Lieutenant?"

"Yes, certainly."

"You did so find a bloody imprint on the tread of the companionway?"

"Yes."

"Have you ever ascertained . . ."

"If the Court please," Burger interrupted, "this isn't proper cross-examination. I'd like to put on my case in an orderly manner. I'd like to introduce in evidence a shoe belonging to the defendant, Carol Burbank. Then I'd like to show the bloodstain on that shoe. And *then* I would like to show the fact of the bloodstain on the tread of the companionway."

"But if Mr. Mason wants to interrogate the witness on that point on cross-examination, I see no reason why he should be bound by the manner in which you choose to introduce your evidence or present your case," the Court ruled. "This witness is a police officer. The defense certainly is entitled to cross-examine him in detail. Moreover, you should now bring out all he knows, not put on your case piecemeal."

"I intended to prove the footprint by another witness, Your Honor."

"But the point now is, does *this* witness know about that print?"

"He seems to."

"Then let him tell what he knows," the judge snapped. "The Court wants to get on with the case, not have matters delayed so the prosecution can build to a dramatic climax. This witness is a police officer. On cross-examination, the defense will have the utmost latitude. The objection is overruled. The witness will answer the question."

"Yes," Tragg said defiantly, "such an imprint was left on the tread of the companionway, and it happens that I have the shoe with which that print was made."

"Exactly," Mason said. "Now let's look at the photograph, People's Exhibit No. Five. I call your attention to a candle which appears in that exhibit. Do you notice it?"

"I know there was a candle there."

"Well, take a good look at this photograph," Mason said, "and study that candle carefully."

"Yes sir, I see it."

"Is there anything about the appearance of that candle which impresses you as being at all unusual?"

"No, sir. It is simply a candle fastened to the top of a table in the cabin of the yacht where the body was found."

"How much of that candle has been burnt?"

"About one inch, perhaps a little less."

"And have you made any experiments to ascertain how long it took a candle of this nature to consume approximately one inch of its length when it was ignited under circumstances similar to those found in the cabin of this yacht?"

"No sir, I haven't. I didn't deem it necessary."

"Why?"

"Because that candle doesn't mean anything."

"Why doesn't it mean anything, Lieutenant?"

"Because we know when Milfield died and we know how he died. And he was dead long before it got dark, so that candle doesn't mean a thing."

Mason said, "You'll notice that this candle is inclined somewhat from the perpendicular, Lieutenant."

"Yes, I've noticed that."

"Have you taken a protractor, and measured the angle at which that is inclined?"

"No."

"As a matter of fact, isn't it inclined at eighteen degrees from the perpendicular?"

"Well—to tell you the truth, I don't know."

"It appears to you to be about eighteen degrees from the perpendicular?"

"It may be, yes."

"And have you made any attempt to account for the angle at which this candle is leaning?"

Tragg smiled and said, "Only that if the murderer in his haste stuck the candle to the top of the table so that he could see to commit a murder by daylight, then he must

148

have been in too much of a hurry to get the candle straight."

"You haven't any other theory?"

"What other theory could there be?"

Mason smiled and said, "That's all, Lieutenant."

Burger frowned across at Mason. "What's that crooked candle got to do with it?" he asked.

Mason said, "That's my defense."

"Your defense?"

"Yes."

Burger hesitated a moment, then announced ponderously, "Well, it won't hold a candle to the theory I have."

There was laughter from the courtroom.

Mason joined in the laughter, then, as it subsided, said quickly, "You've heard of candling an egg, Mr. District Attorney? Well, I'm candling your case. And it's rotten."

The judge pounded sharply with the gavel. "Counsel will refrain from these personalities and comments on extraneous matters. Call your next witness, Mr. Burger."

"Mr. Arthur St. Claire," Burger said.

The man who came forward to the witness stand and held up his hand to be sworn was a smiling, suave, self-possessed man in the late forties.

Della Street whispered to Perry Mason, "That's the man who was in the taxicab with us. The one who did all the talking about San Francisco. You want to watch him. He's clever."

Mason nodded.

Arthur St. Claire took the stand, testified that he was a member of the police department of the City of Los Angeles in the plain-clothes division, and then looked attentively and courteously at the district attorney waiting for the next question.

"Are you acquainted with the defendant, Carol Burbank?"

"Yes, sir."

"Did you see her on Sunday, the day after the body of Fred Milfield was discovered?"

149

"I did, yes, sir."

"Where?"

"At several places," the man said, and smiled.

"What do you mean by that?"

"I was assigned to shadow her. I followed her from her residence to several different places."

"To the Union Terminal?" Burger asked.

"Yes, sir. Eventually she went to the Union Terminal, and then from there she went to the Woodridge Hotel."

"Directing your attention to the Union Terminal," Burger said, "did you see anyone join her while she was there?"

"Yes, sir."

"Who?"

"Miss Della Street, the secretary of Perry Mason."

"Ah, ha!" Hamilton Burger said, his tone containing the savage satisfaction of a cat purring over a freshly caught mouse. "And *what* happened after Miss Della Street joined Miss Carol Burbank?"

"They entered a taxicab and were taken to the Woodridge Hotel."

"And where were you while they were in the taxicab?"

The man grinned. "I was right there in the same cab with them."

"And did you hear their conversation?"

"I did."

"And what did they do?"

"They went to the Woodridge Hotel."

"And what happened when they arrived at the Woodridge Hotel?"

"Miss Street stated that she believed Mr. Mason had telephoned to make reservations for them, and the clerk said he had. She registered for both herself and Miss Burbank, using the initials of Miss Burbank, rather than her first name, and not prefacing it with either Miss or Mrs."

"And then what?"

"Then Miss Street took from her purse an envelope

150

addressed to Mr. Perry Mason, and started to hand it to the clerk, stating that Mr. Mason would call for it."

"And then what?"

"Then I stepped forward and advised them that the district attorney wanted to see them, or that they were wanted at Headquarters or something to that effect."

"And then what?"

"And then I took possession of the envelope."

"And what did you do?"

"I opened it."

"And what did you find inside of it?"

"I found a parcel check, one of the numbered slips of pasteboard issued by the checking counter at the Los Angeles Union Terminal."

"Did you do anything to identify that pasteboard claim check so that you would know it if you saw it again?"

"I did."

"What did you do?"

"I wrote my name on it."

"You mean put your own signature on the back of it?"

"Yes."

Hamilton Burger, with something of a flourish, said, "I show you a piece of pasteboard purporting to be a claim check issued from the Parcel Checking Service at the Los Angeles Terminal, and which contains the name written on the back of it in ink, 'Arthur St. Claire,' and ask you if that is your signature."

"It is, yes, sir."

"And is this the claim check that was in that envelope?"

"It is."

"The claim check that Della Street then and there left at the Woodridge Hotel and in connection with which she stated Mr. Mason would call?"

"Yes, sir."

"This was in an envelope which contained the name of Mr. Perry Mason on the outside?"

"Yes, sir."

"I show you an envelope addressed in pen and ink handwriting, 'Mr. Perry Mason, City,' and ask you if that is the envelope in which this claim check was found."

"It is."

"That is the envelope which Miss Della Street handed to the clerk in the Woodridge Hotel at that time?"

"She started to hand it to him. I took it from her just before the clerk took possession of it."

"And you went to the Los Angeles Terminal with that claim check?"

"I did, yes, sir."

"And presented it?"

"Yes, sir."

"And what did you receive?"

"A package."

"Did you open that package?"

"Not at the time. I took it to Police Headquarters and it was opened there."

"But you were present when it was opened?"

"Yes."

"And what was in it?"

"A pair of shoes."

"Would you recognize those shoes if you saw them again?"

"I would, yes, sir."

"Are these the shoes?" Burger asked, producing a pair of shoes.

The witness inspected them. "They are, yes, sir."

"Did you make any examination of those shoes at that time for the purpose of determining whether there was any foreign substance on them?"

"I did, yes, sir."

"And what did you find?"

"I found reddish stains which resembled dried blood between the sole of the shoe and the upper."

"You don't know whether those stains actually were blood or not?"

The witness said, "I was present at the time when the laboratory expert completed his examination and pronounced . . ."

"Never mind, never mind," Burger interrupted with a fine show of impartiality. "Mr. Mason would object that this was hearsay evidence, and we'll just do everything in a regular and orthodox manner. We'll call the laboratory expert and let *him* testify as to what he found. All *you* can testify to is what *you* know."

"Yes, sir."

"And that's all you know?"

"Yes, sir."

"Cross-examine," Burger said triumphantly.

Mason studied Arthur St. Claire for a few moments. The witness turned to face the defense lawyer with every exterior evidence of affable courtesy, showing an attentive interest in the questions Mason was about to ask.

"You were shadowing Carol Burbank?" Mason asked.

"Yes sir, that's right."

"And were you, or were you not alone on that job?"

The witness hesitated. "There was another man with me," he said at length, and his voice had lost some of its assurance.

"Who was that man?"

"A detective."

"From the Homicide Squad?"

"From the plain-clothes division."

"What was his name?"

The witness glanced at Hamilton Burger. Burger said promptly, "I object, Your Honor. Incompetent, irrelevant, and immaterial—not proper cross-examination."

"Overruled," the judge snapped.

"What was his name?" Mason asked.

"Harvey Teays."

"And he and you together shadowed the defendant, Carol Burbank, that Sunday?"

"Yes, sir."

"He was present with you at the Union Terminal?"

"Yes, sir."

"And where is he now?"

"Why, I don't know."

"When did you see him last?"

"I can't remember that."

"Now when you say that you don't know where Mr. Teays is, what do you mean?"

"Exactly what I say. I don't know where he is."

"Yes? You mean you don't know *exactly* where he is at this particular moment of your own knowledge, don't you?"

"Well . . . Well yes, naturally."

"Do you know whether Teays is still in the employ of the police department?"

"Well, I think he is."

"Do you *know* that he is?"

"Not of my own knowledge, no."

"As a matter of fact," Mason said, "Mr. Teays left on his vacation, and told you he was going on his vacation, and he told you *where* he was going, didn't he?"

St. Claire twisted uneasily in the chair. "Well . . . I don't know what anybody tells me. I can only testify about things I know of my own knowledge."

"But that's a fact, isn't it?"

"Objected to as incompetent, irrelevant, and immaterial," Maurice Linton said. "The witness is absolutely right. Counsel has no right to call for hearsay testimony."

Judge Newark said somewhat irritably, "Your objection comes too late. If you had objected before this witness had stated he didn't know where Mr. Teays was, there might have been something to the point, but after the witness has stated positively that he doesn't know where he is, Counsel certainly has a right to show what he meant by that answer, and the means of information that are available to the witness. Moreover, some of this shows possible bias."

"I don't see why," Linton objected.

"It shows the animosity of the witness," the judge snapped. "It would have been a very simple matter for the witness to have told Counsel that he didn't know where Mr. Teays was, but did understand that Mr. Teays had left on his vacation. I don't know the object of this cross-examination, but it's quite apparent that Counsel is having to drag the information out of this witness. He shouldn't have to do that on a pertinent fact—not from an officer of the law."

"Do you know *why* Mr. Teays left on his vacation?"

"He wanted to get away from the routine of his work, the same way anyone wants to leave on a vacation."

"Isn't this rather an unusual time to take a vacation?"

"I wouldn't know."

"Do you know whether Mr. Teays intended to take a vacation Sunday when he was working with you on this case?"

"No. I don't."

"He didn't say anything to you about it?"

"No."

"Then suddenly he decided to take his vacation. Do you have any idea why?"

"I've told you all I know about that."

"As a matter of fact," Mason said, "didn't Mr. Teays decide to take his vacation because *he* had picked up the claim check in question and because *he* had given it to Miss Street?"

"I don't know."

"But do you know that Teays did pick up the claim check and give it to Miss Street?"

"Well . . . I couldn't swear that, no."

"Why can't you swear it?"

"I didn't see the claim check—not closely enough to recognize it."

Mason said with an air of dogged persistence, "Let's get at it this way. You were shadowing Carol Burbank every minute of the time there at the Union Terminal?"

"Yes."

"You saw her and Miss Street walk toward the taxi stand?"

"Yes."

"You saw Miss Burbank open her purse and an oblong of pasteboard flutter out to the floor?"

"Well . . . Yes."

"And you saw Mr. Teays pick that pasteboard oblong up and hand it to Miss Street?"

"She reached for it."

"But Teays picked it up and handed it to her?"

"Yes."

"And the only reason you now say you don't know it was this same claim check is because you weren't close enough to read the number on it? Is that right?"

"Well, I can't swear it was this claim check unless I *know* it's the same, can I?"

"It was a piece of pasteboard about this size?"

"Yes."

"Approximately of this appearance?"

"Yes."

"With perforated edges along one side?"

"Well . . . Yes."

"And had a large number printed on it? You saw that much?"

"Yes."

"How close were you to Teays when he picked it up?"

"Eight or ten feet."

"Did Teays tell you he'd handed Miss Street that claim check?"

"Objected to as improper cross-examination, as incompetent, irrelevant, and immaterial and as calling for hearsay testimony," Linton objected vociferously. "Mr. Teays isn't on trial. Any statement Mr. Teays made to this witness has no bearing on the case. He can only testify to what he saw."

Judge Newark said, "I'm going to sustain that objection. Does the prosecutor's office have any knowledge of why Mr. Teays happened to take his vacation at this particular time?"

"I believe he had two weeks coming," Linton said.

"Do you know when the decision was reached that he would take his vacation now?"

"No, Your Honor, I don't," Linton said.

"Any further questions?" Judge Newark asked Perry Mason.

"None, Your Honor."

Judge Newark frowned at the witness, started to say something, then changed his mind and said to the prosecutors, "Very well, call your next witness. That's all, Mr. St. Claire."

"Dr. Colfax C. Newbern," Linton announced.

Dr. Newbern was a tall, self-possessed individual who took the stand and stated his full name, address and occupation in a low voice to the court reporter, his manner that of calm, professional competence.

"I will stipulate the doctor's qualification as an expert, subject to the right of cross-examination," Mason said.

"Very well," Linton announced. "You are, I believe, attached to the coroner's office, Doctor?"

"That's right."

"I show you a photograph and ask you if you recognize that photograph?"

"I do. That is a photograph of a body upon which I performed an autopsy."

"When did you first see this body, Doctor?"

"I was present when the police boarded the yacht and saw the body lying on the floor of the cabin."

"When did you next see it after that?"

"Sunday morning when I performed an autopsy."

"What was the cause of death, Doctor?"

"The man had received a blow—a very severe blow on the back of the head. There had been a fracture of the skull and a very extensive hemorrhage. I'm trying to put this in common everyday terms so the layman will understand it."

"Quite right, Doctor. Now just tell us a little more about the cause of death, and the time of death."

"In my opinion," Dr. Newbern said, "unconsciousness was an immediate result of that blow. The victim never regained consciousness and, judging from the extent of the hemorrhage and the conditions I found in the brain, I would say that death occurred within five minutes."

"In your opinion then, the victim never moved from the time that blow was struck?"

"That's right."

"Now when you first saw the body, Doctor, where was it with reference to the surroundings shown in this photograph which I now hand you?"

"The body was over here," the doctor said, indicating a point on the photograph. "It was way over on the right-hand side of the boat. That is, what is referred to in nautical terms as starboard side. It is the right side when you face the bow. This photograph was taken looking toward the stern of the boat. Therefore, the position where the body was found would have been in the left-hand portion of this photograph."

"I'll show you a photograph, People's Exhibit C, which actually shows a body and ask you if that is approximately the position and location of the body when you first saw it."

"That is exactly the position and location of the body, yes, sir. That is the body as it was lying when I first saw it."

"Did you make any examination of the premises when the body was discovered?"

"Not when the body was discovered," the doctor corrected with a smile, "but when the police arrived."

"You did make such an examination?"

"Yes."

"What did you discover?"

Dr. Newbern said, "I discovered the body lying in approximately this position which, you will notice, is face up on the starboard side of the yacht. I noticed that under the head there was a pool of blood indicating a rather extensive hemorrhage. I also noticed that at another point in the cabin, the carpet was saturated with blood. Do you wish me to point that out?"

"Please."

"That was in approximately here."

Mason, getting up to walk around behind the witness so he could see the point the witness fixed on the photograph, said, "If the Court please, for the sake of the record, the doctor is now pointing to a portion of the photograph, People's Exhibit C, which is in the upper right-hand corner and immediately in front of the doorway which enters the after cabin of the yacht. That's right, Doctor?"

"That's right," the doctor said.

"Thank you," Mason announced and returned to his seat.

"You noticed there was a pool of blood here?" Linton continued.

"Yes, sir. And there were a few small bloodstains at more or less regular intervals between these two spots."

"Did you make any examination of the threshold between the main cabin and the after cabin?"

"I did, yes, sir."

"What did you find?"

"I found that the threshold was raised approximately three inches, as is, I believe, usual in yacht construction. I found that the threshold was covered with brass, and that there were spots of discoloration on this brass. I made scrapings of those discolorations and determined that they were human blood. I typed the blood and found that it was of the same type of blood as that of the body which was found in the position which I have indicated on the floor."

"The point at which you have testified the body was found was a distance of several feet from that threshold?" Linton asked.

"Yes, sir."

"Was there anything to indicate how that body might have been moved from the one spot, which we will refer to as position number one, to the other, which we will refer to as position number two?"

"Yes, sir."

"What?"

"The force of gravitation could well have moved that body," Dr. Newbern said smiling.

"Will you please explain?"

"When we boarded the yacht, it was almost low tide. The yacht had heeled way over until it was very difficult to keep one's footing. The boat was tilted so that the starboard side was the low side, and so far as the medical evidence is concerned, it is quite apparent that as the tide had gone out the night before, the body had rolled over into approximately the position in which it was found."

"The body could have done that without being touched by any person?"

"In my opinion the body would have done that without being touched *if* the period of low tide had preceded rigor mortis. If the body had been lying with the arms and legs outspread, and rigor mortis had set in before the interval of low tide, it is quite possible the body would not have moved very much from its original position. But with a low tide intervening before rigor mortis set in, the body would very naturally have rolled over to the low part of the cabin."

"When does rigor mortis set in?"

"As a rule, general stiffening will be well established within ten hours after death. Say ten to twelve hours to make a pretty fair average."

"Rigor mortis had developed in the body at the time you saw it?"

"Oh yes."

"And what time was that?"

"That was eleven-seventeen Saturday morning."

"In your opinion, Doctor, what was the time of death?"

"The time of death," Dr. Newbern said, "was from fourteen to eighteen hours before I first examined the body."

"Can you fix that in terms of hours?"

"I examined the body at eleven-seventeen. I would, therefore, say that death occurred after five-seventeen the previous evening, and before nine-seventeen. Any time within that four-hour limit would satisfy the conditions as I observed them."

"The nature of the wound was such that it caused rather extensive hemorrhage?"

"Both external and internal, yes. There was a rather severe hemorrhage."

"In your opinion, death was almost instantaneous?"

"I would say from the conditions which I observed that in this particular case unconsciousness followed immediately upon the blow, and death occurred within an interval of a few minutes."

"Were there any other wounds on the body?"

"There was a contusion on the point of the jaw, just to the left of the point."

"Indicating a blow?"

"Indicating a trauma of some sort. There was a well-defined traumatic ecchymosis."

"Any other wounds on the body?"

"None whatever."

"Cross-examine," Linton said. "He's your witness."

Mason slowly got to his feet, faced the doctor. "Then this wound, which we will describe as the fatal wound, is the only one which would have caused any hemorrhage?"

161

"That's right."

"Now then, Doctor, how long would hemorrhage from such a wound continue after death?"

"From this particular wound, I would say that any extensive hemorrhage would have ceased within a very few minutes after death."

"What do you mean by a very few minutes?"

"Well, to be on the safe side, say ten or fifteen minutes."

"On moving the body would there have been another drainage of blood?"

"Yes, sir. That's right."

"And how long would that have continued?"

"That would have continued for some time."

"Then the pool which you found under the head of the body in the position in which you found it might have been the result of drainage from moving the body?"

"No, sir, I don't think so. There were evidences of a true hemorrhage rather than mere drainage. And from the size, the nature and the extent of that stain on the carpet, I would say that it was the result of hemorrhage."

"You aren't, however, taking that into consideration in fixing the time of death?"

"In fixing the time of death," Dr. Newbern said, "I am acting only upon the evidence which I found in my examination of the body itself. As far as my examination of the environment of the body, that is a matter for the detective. I am testifying here only as an expert medical witness. I am fixing the time of death from various evidences as to the body temperature, the onset of rigor mortis, and the state of progress of certain other very definite post-mortem changes. I am not engaging in any detective work or any speculation predicated upon the position of the body other than as that position has some medical significance."

"I see. That is, of course, a very conservative and a very proper position for you to take, Doctor."

"Thank you."

"I take it, Doctor, that there was every evidence that the blow which caused death was a severe one?"

"The blow was very severe."

"In your opinion, could that blow have been sustained by a man stumbling and falling back against the threshold?"

"I doubt it very much. In my opinion, that blow was very severe. *If* it was sustained when the head was thrown against that threshold, then the blow must have been more severe than would have been the case if it had been sustained in an ordinary fall occasioned through stumbling. The man must have been knocked back against that threshold with very considerable force."

"A force which could have resulted from a blow?"

"That could have done it, yes—a blow struck by a very powerful man."

"Then it is possible that the victim could have been struck on the point of the chin at the place where you saw that bruise, and the force of that blow would have thrown him back against the threshold and inflicted the injury which caused his death?"

"That's objected to," Linton said, "as incompetent, irrelevant and immaterial and improper cross-examination. It assumes a fact not in evidence, and is a frantic attempt by the defense to secure some peg upon which it can hang—a defense of manslaughter."

"Objection overruled," Judge Newark said. "The defense is entitled to cross-examine any witness upon any theory he sees fit, just so that theory is pertinent to the issues, and the questions cover matters which directly or by inference were touched upon in the examination in chief. Answer the question, Doctor."

"That *could* have been the case."

"It is possible?"

"It is possible."

"That's all."

Linton said, "Just a minute, Doctor. Inasmuch as this element has been injected into the case, while you say that it is *possible* that the injury could have been received in such a manner, assuming for the sake of this question that it had been received in such a manner, what would have been the nature of that blow?"

"It would have been a very violent blow. The man must have been struck in such a manner that much of the force of that blow was transmitted to the impact of the head against the threshold. In other words, the head must have struck with greater force than would have been the result of an ordinary fall."

"A blow that would have taken the injured person entirely off guard?"

"Well, a very violent blow."

"Not a blow which would have been struck in a combat where the recipient was braced, but a blow which was struck in such a manner that the recipient was caught entirely off guard—is that right?"

"That isn't at all what I said," the doctor answered. "I am not an expert on fighting," he added with a faint smile. "I am only an expert on medical matters."

"But that seems to be a necessary inference to be drawn from your testimony," Linton insisted.

"Draw it then," the doctor announced in a dry, crisp voice. "It is an inference for you to draw. I am only stating the conditions as I found them."

"But the blow must have necessarily been very violent?"

"It took a very great amount of force to cause the injury which I have described."

"But can't you tell us any more than that, Doctor?"

"I can only repeat that it was not the type of injury one would expect to find from the striking of the head caused in an ordinary fall such as is occasioned when a person loses balance. It was an injury that was caused by an impact occasioned by considerable violence. That is not exactly the way I wish to express it, either, Counselor. I will say that under the circumstances which we are now discussing, and the possibility which is being considered in my testimony, the head of the deceased must have struck the threshold with greater force than would have been the result of an ordinary fall. That's as far as I care to go, and I think that's as clear as I can make it."

"In the event that force which contributed to the fall had been a blow, it would have been a heavy blow?" Linton asked.

"Yes."

"A blow struck by a trained fighter?"

"I cannot swear to that."

"But definitely a blow that was very violent?"

"In the generally accepted, popular meaning of the word, yes."

"I think that's all," Linton said.

"That's all," Mason announced.

"Call your next witness," the judge said.

"Thomas Lawton Cameron," Linton announced.

Thomas L. Cameron turned out to be a weather-beaten man in the late fifties, broad-shouldered, stocky, competent, with a face covered with a fine network of wrinkles from which steady eyes regarded the world in an intent scrutiny from under black, bushy eyebrows. He was, it transpired, a caretaker at the yacht club where Roger Burbank kept his yacht, and he answered questions in a low-pitched voice, wasting no words, most of the time answering questions in a frank, conversational manner.

Cameron testified that it was Burbank's custom to take his yacht out over week-ends; that usually he left on Friday about noon; that on the particular Friday in question he had arrived at the yacht club about eleven-thirty; that he had boarded his yacht, cast loose the moorings, hoisted sail, jockeyed the yacht out into the channel and sailed around the point and up the lagoon or estuary,

165

whichever you wanted to call it. That he had then, within an hour, returned in the yacht's dinghy powered with an outboard motor, had tied the dinghy up and had been away all afternoon. That sometime around five o'clock the witness had heard the noise of the outboard motor and had glanced out of the window of his cabin workshop. He had seen the yacht's dinghy chugging down toward the main estuary. There was someone in the stern, but the witness wasn't prepared to state this person was the defendant. He hadn't seen the figure clearly enough to identify it.

"Are you acquainted with the deceased, Fred Milfield?" Linton asked.

"Yes."

"Did you see him that Friday afternoon?"

"I did."

"When?"

"He arrived at the yacht club about five-thirty and rented a rowboat from me."

"You're certain it was Fred Milfield?"

"Yes."

"Was there some mark of identification on this rowboat?"

"Yes, a number."

"What was the number?"

"Twenty-five."

"When did you next see this rowboat?"

"Almost twenty-four hours later. We found it Saturday afternoon where it had run aground after having been carried by the tide."

"Where did it run aground?"

"Up the estuary, about half a mile below where Burbank's yacht was anchored."

"*Below* the spot where the yacht was anchored?"

"Yes."

"So the boat must have been cast loose while the tide was running out—sometime after high tide?"

166

"Well—I guess that's a matter of deduction."

"Did you see Burbank any more after that?"

"Yes. I saw him come back in his dinghy about half or three-quarters of an hour after Milfield left. He tied it up to the mooring, went over to his car, and drove away."

"Did you see him again later?"

"Well, I didn't see him. It was when I was answering the phone; someone started an outboard motor. I heard the putt-putt as the boat went past, but I was busy talking, and I didn't look out. After I finished my telephone conversation, I looked out and the Burbank dinghy was gone. It was getting dark when it came back, and so I never did see who was in it."

"Then what happened to this dinghy?"

"Well, as near as I can tell, it remained tied up all night. I didn't hear anyone start the outboard motor. If anyone had, I think I'd have waked up. I didn't. I slept right through after I got to bed. That was around midnight. The dinghy was there when I went to bed, and it was there when I got up in the morning, around six o'clock."

"When did you next see Milfield?"

"That was after this sheepherder came rushing in . . ."

"Never mind the hearsay," Linton interrupted. "I just want to know when you next saw Mr. Milfield."

"Saturday morning."

"That was the day following the occurrences of which you have just testified?"

"Yes, sir."

"And where was Mr. Milfield?"

"His body was lying aboard Roger Burbank's yacht."

"Were you alone at the time you saw him?"

"No, sir. Lieutenant Tragg was with me, and a couple of other gentlemen whose names I have forgotten."

"Police officers?"

"I believe so, yes."

"Was Mr. Milfield alive or dead?"

167

"He was dead."

"You may cross-examine," Linton announced to Perry Mason.

"Did you actually see Roger Burbank return to the club in that dinghy?" Mason asked.

"Yes, sure."

"Talk with him?"

"No."

"See him get in his car and drive away?"

"Yes."

"Saw him clearly?"

"As clearly as you could see a man at that distance."

"How far was it?"

"Oh, perhaps a hundred and fifty feet."

"You were wearing your glasses at the time?"

"Yes, sure."

"Know it was Burbank in that dinghy as soon as you saw him?"

"Well, to tell the truth—I sort of took it for granted when I *first* saw the man that it was someone else."

"Milfield?"

"Yes."

"Now how far away was this?"

"Like I told you, it was right around a hundred and fifty feet, or two hundred feet."

"*Where* were you?"

"In my little cabin, down there."

"What were you doing?"

"Cooking dinner."

"Have your glasses on?"

"Yes."

"Looked out through a window?"

"Yes."

"And saw this man?"

"Yes."

"There may have been some steam on your glasses—from the cooking?"

"Well there *may* have been. It's a chance."

"And," Mason said, pointing his finger to give added emphasis to his words, "at the time, you thought this man was Fred Milfield, didn't you?"

"Yes, I did."

"When did you first realize that it wasn't Fred Milfield?"

"When I saw Milfield dead there in Roger Burbank's yacht."

Mason said, "And you first told the officers that Milfield came back in the yacht's dinghy. It was when the officers pointed out to you that it was an impossibility for Milfield to have done so, because Milfield was lying dead on Roger Burbank's yacht, that you decided the man whom you had seen in the dinghy was Roger Burbank. Isn't that right?"

"Yes, sir. I guess when you come right down to it, that's right."

Mason said, "It was Roger Burbank's habit to take his yacht out Friday at noon?"

"Yes, sir. He used his yacht just to get away from people."

"Did Fred Milfield join him on occasion?"

"Well, yes, Mr. Milfield did, and perhaps once or twice during the year Mr. Beltin would come out, but only when there was something terribly important. Mr. Burbank didn't like it."

"How do you know he didn't?"

"He told me so. He told me he'd got that yacht so that he could get away from everything. He said that now he couldn't get gasoline, he had this sailboat, and he'd sail out just a mile or so up the estuary and anchor on the mud flats. He said the minute he got out of sight of the yacht club, he felt like a new man. He felt as though he was off all by himself."

"You say he anchored on the mud flats?"

"Yes. He liked to spear sharks."

"Would he keep the boat anchored on the mud flats?"

"No, sir. He'd just anchor it there a couple of hours before high tide, and keep it there for maybe a couple of hours after high tide."

"Why?"

"Well, out on those mud flats the water gets pretty shallow around low tide, and a boat would go on the ground if you left it there during low tide."

"That wouldn't necessarily hurt anything, however?"

"No, sir. Not unless a wind came up. If a wind came up a boat could get a nasty pounding there."

"Even in such shallow water?" Mason asked.

The witness smiled and said, "Shallow water would give it the worst pounding. You see, the waves would build up enough so the crests would pick it up off the mud, and then when the troughs of the waves came along, the boat would slam down on the mud. A boat that's slap aground in no water at all is all right. A boat that's floating is all right. But you take a boat that's aground in shallow water where waves can build up, and that boat's going to take a terrific beating."

"Well then, where would Mr. Burbank go during periods of low tide?"

"He'd anchor out in the channel just fifty or a hundred yards away from the place where he usually speared his sharks."

"Now on this Friday night, do you know when the tide was low?"

"Yes, sir."

"When?"

"Well now, I can't give you the exact hour and minute, but it was high tide right around five-forty, somewhere around there. It might have been five-forty-one or perhaps five-forty-five, but that wouldn't miss it a minute or so. Make it five-forty, and you won't miss it two minutes either way."

"That was high tide?"

"Yes, sir."

"And when," Mason asked, "was low tide?"

"Low tide was at three minutes past midnight on Saturday."

"Then," Mason said, "if anyone had been going to move the yacht away from those mud flats, the yacht would necessarily have been moved within two hours of high tide? And that would mean by seven-forty in the evening?"

"Well, not necessarily. I'd say you could have got off—well, say up until eight o'clock. That would be the limit."

"And if you didn't get off by eight o'clock you wouldn't get off?" Mason asked.

"That's right. Not until a couple of hours before the next high tide."

"And when was the next high tide?"

"Six-twenty-six a. m. Saturday morning."

"And when was the next low tide after that?"

"Twelve-forty-five Saturday. That's how the body came to be discovered."

"You might tell me a little more about that," Mason said.

"Well, it was along about ten o'clock in the morning. I guess it was. And the boat had begun to settle a little on the mud bank. Maybe around ten-thirty."

"Now by the boat, you mean the yacht?" Mason asked.

"That's right. Roger Burbank's yacht."

"All right," Mason said. "Go ahead. The yacht had begun to settle on the mud, and what happened?"

"Well, it seemed some man by the name of Palermo had an appointment with Milfield, and . . ."

"This is all the rankest sort of hearsay," Linton interrupted.

"Do you want to object to it?" Mason asked.

"I don't wish to be put in the position of objecting to anything so trivial."

Mason said to the judge, "Some of this is probably hearsay, Your Honor, but I'm simply trying to get a picture of what happened, and get it in the most expeditious manner."

"But we're going to call Frank Palermo, the witness who discovered the body," Linton argued. "You can ask Palermo what he saw."

"I'm not going to ask this man about what Palermo saw," Mason said. "I'm going to ask him about when he met Palermo and what Palermo said. And I'm simply asking him about these other matters so that we can clarify the situation and have a clear picture before the court. I want to present a chronological sequence of events."

"And why do you want to clutter up the record with a lot of testimony about what Palermo was doing *after* he discovered the body?" Linton asked.

"Because," Mason said, smiling, "I might uncover some fact that was favorable to the defense."

Linton said sarcastically, *"This* witness doesn't know anything favorable to the defense, and no other witness who gets on the stand and *tells* the truth will know anything that's favorable to the defense. No one knows anything favorable to the defense."

"If he did," Mason observed, "he'd probably be taking his vacation."

A roar of laughter was silenced by Judge Newark's gavel. "Counsel will refrain from these side comments. Do you wish to make an objection, Mr. Linton?"

"No, I'm not going to be put in the position of objecting to this testimony, Your Honor."

"If Counsel for the People doesn't object, the Court will hear enough of it to get the general background," the judge ruled. "Go ahead and answer the question."

"I'll put it this way," Mason said. "You were the first

person to talk with the man who had discovered the body?"

"I believe so, yes."

"Tell us exactly what happened."

"Well, it was Saturday morning around ten-thirty, I guess. I didn't look at the time. And I saw this boat coming up the estuary with a man standing up sculling."

"Anything that directed your attention to this boat particularly?"

"Yes."

"What?"

"The way the man was sculling."

"And what about it?"

"All this is incompetent, irrelevant and immaterial. It has no bearing whatever on the case," Linton objected.

"Overruled."

"Well, there aren't very many people that can make a really good job of sculling a boat, and this man was sculling right along. That boat was really cutting through the water. And another thing that interested me was the type of boat."

"What sort of a boat was it?" Mason asked.

"It was a folding boat—one that is made to be folded and carried in an automobile."

"And who was the man in the boat?"

"When he came closer, he started to talk—all excited— a lot of foreign accent—said his name was Frank Palermo, that he was from up in the Skinner Hills district, and that he had an appointment with Milfield on a yacht, and . . ."

"This is all hearsay," Linton pointed out.

"Are you objecting to it?"

"Yes, Your Honor, I'm going to object to this as hearsay evidence, and as not proper cross-examination. This man is . . ."

"Sustained," Judge Newark ruled.

"All right," Mason said to the witness, "just confine yourself generally to what you did."

"Well, this man made some statements to me about what he'd found, and as a result of those statements, I communicated with the police."

"Now what did you tell the police?"

"Same objection," Linton said.

"Overruled," the judge snapped. "Witness is now being cross-examined as to something he said and did himself."

"Well, I telephoned Police Headquarters and told them . . ."

"Never mind what you told them," Linton said.

"On the contrary," Mason announced, "I'm interested in what the witness told the police. I believe this is part of the *res gestae,* and in any event, it will show possible bias."

"The objection is overruled."

"Well, I told the police that I was caretaker and watchman at the yacht club, and that some crazy foreigner was claiming that he had an appointment with Milfield . . ."

"Your Honor," Linton protested, "this is exactly the same matter which the Court refused to permit the witness to testify to earlier."

"Oh, no, it isn't," the judge said. "At that time he was testifying as to what Palermo had told him. Now he's testifying as to what *he* told the police. The defense is certainly entitled to cross-examine this witness as to what he said and did in connection with this matter—if it wants to show bias."

"But Counsel is going to get it all in just the same," Linton protested, "because this man is now about to relate his conversation with the police over the telephone."

"Let him relate it then," Judge Newark said. "The objection is overruled."

"Go ahead," Mason said, "answer the question."

"Well, I told the police that this man Palermo was there in a boat; that he said he'd had an appointment on Burbank's yacht with Fred Milfield; that when he went out there to where Milfield had told him the yacht would be, he found it heeled well over on its side, aground on a mud bar. He sculled his boat around it and shouted a couple of times . . ."

Linton said desperately, "I want the witness to understand that he is only to testify as to what he told the police and not what Palermo told him."

Cameron said, "I'm telling about what I told the police Palermo told me. Isn't that all right?"

Judge Newark smiled, "That's all right. Go right ahead."

"Well, I said that Palermo said he'd sculled around the yacht a couple of times and then he'd boarded it and called out to find if anyone was aboard. And when he received no answer, he slid back the hatch and went down into the cabin and found Fred Milfield lying dead."

"Any further conversation?" Mason asked.

"That was about all."

"Any conversation between you and the police about Palermo?"

"Well, a little. Yes. It seems the police knew who I was and wanted to know if Palermo had rented a boat from me."

"And what did you tell them?"

The witness smiled. "I told them just what Palermo told me when I asked him where he got the boat."

"And what was that?"

"Palermo don't seem to believe in squandering money. He said he knew that he was going to have to row out to a yacht on the estuary; and since he already had this folding boat for use on the Skinner Hills Lake in taking out duck-shooting parties, he saw no reason to pay some city slicker fifty cents or a dollar for boat rental, so he simply loaded his folding boat into his automobile and used that to go out to the yacht."

"I don't see what possible bearing this has on the case," Linton said.

Mason smiled, "It might be a fact favorable to the defense."

"Well, I don't see it."

"That," Mason announced with mock sympathy, "is the result of a legal astigmatism."

"Come, come, gentlemen, let's get on with the case," Judge Newark said.

"Did you," Mason asked, "tell the police anything that Palermo told you about the time he had left his residence in Skinner Hills in order to keep his appointment?"

"He told me something about that, but I didn't tell the police."

"Then the witness obviously can't testify to it," Linton said.

"And the witness obviously isn't being asked about it," Mason announced.

"Proceed," Judge Newark said, somewhat tartly.

"You rent rowboats?" Mason asked.

"Yes, sir. That's right."

"Is there any other place nearby that rents rowboats?"

"No, sir. I think mine is the only place at present where boats can be rented."

"Now then, did you rent any boats on the Friday night when the murder was committed?"

"That also is objected to as not being proper cross-examination."

"Overruled."

"Answer the question, Mr. Cameron."

"I rented one rowboat."

"Only one?"

"Yes, sir."

"What period of time are you including in your answer?"

"From four o'clock in the afternoon on until after the body was discovered."

"To whom was this boat rented?"

Cameron smiled. "The man's name was Smith. He put up a deposit of five dollars and rented the boat to make some studies of the nocturnal habits of sharks. At least, that's what he said he wanted to do."

"And what time was this boat rented?" Mason asked.

"The boat was rented at right around nine o'clock in the evening."

"For how long was it rented?"

"He returned it at exactly twenty minutes past ten, about one hour and twenty minutes later. I remember there was some discussion about the length of time he'd been out, and I told him to call it an hour and let it go at that because I couldn't remember whether it had been right on the dot of nine o'clock when he started out or not."

"Wasn't an hour rather a short time to make a study of the nocturnal habits of sharks?"

"It depends on how many habits you want to study— and how many sharks."

There was laughter in the courtroom.

"After all," Linton pointed out, "the witness isn't an expert on the subject of sharks."

Cameron coughed deprecatingly. "It happens," he said, I *am* an expert on sharks. I've studied them."

Judge Newark became interested in this phase of the testimony. "You don't know who this gentleman was?" he asked, leaning forward. "You only knew that his name was Smith?"

"Yes, sir."

"Did you report this to the police?"

"Well . . . I don't believe I did. I don't believe they asked me."

"That's the only rowboat that was rented the night of the murder?"

"Yes."

"From what time did you say?"

"From four o'clock in the afternoon. I rented another boat at three o'clock, but it was back by five."

"To whom was that rented?"

"A woman who was also a stranger."

"A woman who was unaccompanied?"

"That's right. She was doing some fishing, however. I rent quite a few boats for fishing."

"And this man Smith," the judge asked, "can you describe him?"

"Yes, sir, I can. He was a young man, rather dark, very slender, and very much of a greenhorn with a boat. I remember noticing that because it impressed me that . . ."

"I don't think the witness's impressions are pertinent," Linton objected.

"Perhaps not," the judge agreed irritably. "However, the Court is interested in this phase of the witness's testimony. You say that he didn't know much about handling a boat?"

"That's right, Your Honor."

"Wasn't that rather unusual for a man who had taken an interest, even if only an academic interest, in the habits of sharks?"

"That," Cameron replied, "is what I was trying to say when this lawyer stopped me. It impressed me as being strange that a man . . ."

Judge Newark smiled, "I don't think we need your impression now, Mr. Cameron. Can you describe the appearance of this man in any greater detail? How was he dressed? What did he weigh?"

"Well, he was bundled up in an overcoat, and that was another thing that was—well, not exactly strange, but out of place."

"In what way?"

"Well, Your Honor, a person who is going to row a

178

boat will wear a good heavy jacket—a Mackinaw, or a leather coat, or something of that sort, and trousers and shoes or boots. It's very seldom that a man who's around rowboats much wears an overcoat—particularly an overcoat that has any class to it."

"Why?"

"Well, you see rowboats leak—all boats leak some, and usually the bottoms of the boats are more or less messy with fish bait and things of that sort. And an overcoat in a rowboat drags down on the bottom of the boat and gets dirty. You just can't keep an overcoat from doing it. The way a rowboat is constructed, the seat is so low that when a person sits on it, the skirt of the overcoat will drag on the bottom of the boat and in any water that's there."

"Yes, yes. I see your point," Judge Newark said, quite plainly interested now. "And this man was wearing an overcoat. Can you describe the overcoat?"

"It was a light-colored overcoat, sort of a light gray, but it was a good heavy coat."

"Any pattern in it?"

"No, Your Honor."

"And you say he was around thirty?"

"I would say he was right around thirty—probably not over thirty."

"And what about his appearance?"

"Well, I noticed he was rather slender with a dark complexion, and he had a sort of a stoop. I can't describe what I mean exactly, but when you're around the waterfront, if you'll notice people who have worked around yachts or boats, they're nearly always deep-chested. And you take a person who's hollow-chested and he sort of stands out. You notice him."

"I see," Judge Newark said. "Now this man rented the rowboat at about nine o'clock and returned about ten-thirty?"

"Yes, Your Honor, that's correct."

"Did he say anything about where he'd been?"

"Just out on the flat studying sharks. He had a flashlight with him."

"Any notebook?"

"Not that I could see. I don't know what he had in the pocket of his overcoat."

"Did he ask any questions about the location of the mud flats?" Mason asked.

"No, sir, he didn't. He seemed to know right where he was going. He got in the boat and started out. But you could tell that he was a greenhorn from the way he handled the boat."

"How so?"

"Well, his stroke wasn't regular, and he caught a crab now and then. Sometimes his oars would go down deep in the water and sometimes they'd just be breaking through the surface. He didn't—well, he just didn't make any headway. He didn't handle the boat. He didn't seem to know anything about water or about boats."

"And that's the only boat you rented that night?"

"That's right."

"And you'd recognize this man if you saw him again?"

"Yes, sir. I think I would."

"That's all," Judge Newark said to Mason. "Proceed, Counselor."

"Now then," Mason went on, abruptly changing the subject of his cross-examination, "you were waiting for the police when they arrived, is that right?"

"Yes, sir."

"And did you volunteer to take them out to the yacht?"

"Yes, sir. They asked me if I knew where the yacht would be, and I told them I knew right where Mr. Burbank customarily anchored."

"You got out there to the yacht at about what time?"

"Oh, around eleven-fifteen, I guess."

"That was almost at dead low tide?"

"That lacked just about an hour and a half of being dead low tide. That's right, yes, sir."

"And by that time the boat was aground?"

"I'll say it was aground."

"Tilted pretty well over?"

"Tilted way over. You could hardly stand on the thing."

"And that tilting had perhaps disarranged some of the evidence?" Mason asked.

"Well, I don't know about that. I'm not making any statement about the condition of the evidence."

"How far was the boat heeled over?"

"It was heeled way over."

"About how far from the perpendicular?"

"It must have been somewhere around twenty-five to thirty degrees."

"And it was hard to keep your footing under those circumstances?"

"I'll say it was."

"The body was lying on the floor?"

"Yes."

"In the position shown in this photograph?"

"That's right, yes, sir."

"Now then," Mason said, "if the murder took place along in the evening there must have been one other intervening dead low tide. That is, the low tide which occurred at three minutes past twelve on Saturday morning, is that right?"

"Yes, sir."

"And one intervening high tide?"

"Yes, sir."

"What time would that have been?"

"Six-twenty-six a. m. on that Saturday morning."

"You remember the tides?"

"That's my business—part of it. I remember them."

"Now in this photograph," Mason said, "the position in which the body is shown is over on the side of the cabin, with the head lying down against the low corner as shown in the photograph."

"Yes, sir."

"And isn't it quite possible that the body could have rolled from a position at the other end of the cabin?"

"It is, yes, sir."

"During the period of dead low tide which occurred at three minutes past midnight the night before?"

"Yes, sir."

"So that the fact that the position of the body as shown in the photograph might be exactly the same as the position in which it was when the body was discovered, would not preclude the possibility that the body had rolled during the night, during the low tide which occurred three minutes after midnight."

"I'd say that that body was pretty apt to have rolled," the witness said.

"He's not an expert on bodies," Linton objected.

"He's an expert on boats," the judge snapped.

"You take a list like that," the witness explained to the judge, "and you're going to find things at the low side of the cabin. Now on this particular boat, the way she was listed, the starboard side was the low side. The body could have been clean over on the other side of the cabin when the murder was committed, but that dead low tide at twelve-o-three would have rolled her over."

Mason took from his pocket a protractor, walked up to the judge's bench and said, "The Court might care to do a little armchair detective work."

"Thank you," the judge said, smiling. "I was just thinking of that."

"I don't understand this interchange between Court and Counsel," Linton objected.

Judge Newark placed the protractor on the photograph and said, "I think it's—'It's elementary, my dear Watson,'" he added with a smile.

The courtroom broke into audible merriment which the judge made no effort to control.

The discomfited deputy district attorney said, "I think, if the Court please, I'm entitled to an explanation."

"The Court," Judge Newark said, "is doing a little amateur detective work along the lines indicated by Mr. Mason's testimony. You will notice that this candle shown in the photograph is placed on an incline."

"Well, what of it?" Linton asked.

"The protractor shows that the angle of that candle is approximately seventeen degrees from perpendicular."

"All right, what if it is?" Linton said. "Whenever a murderer hastily puts a candle into position, he doesn't use a plumb bob, or a square to make certain that he's got it lined exactly straight up and down."

"What I think you overlooked," Judge Newark said, "and the point which I'm quite certain is in Mr. Mason's mind, is that the wax which has run down from this candle seems to be quite evenly distributed on each side of the candle."

"Well, what's that got to do with it?" Linton demanded. "The wax would run down on both sides equally, wouldn't it?"

"Not if the candle were on a slant," Judge Newark said with a smile. "The candle itself is mute testimony of the fact that when it was burning the candle was in a perpendicular position."

"But how could that be?" Linton said. "You can look at that photograph and it shows the candle well out of the perpendicular."

"Exactly," Judge Newark said. "And I think Mr. Mason's point is, that because the candle is out of perpendicular, it is very good evidence as to the time when the candle was lit. That is your point, Mr. Mason?"

"Exactly," Mason said. "That's why the evidence in connection with these tides is so important."

Judge Newark studied the photograph for a few moments, then said, "It's approaching the hour of five o'clock, and the Court is going to take its evening adjournment. Court will reconvene at ten o'clock tomorrow morning. And in the meantime, the Court suggests that the officers check their theory of the case with the evidence of this tilted candle and the evidence Mr. Mason has brought out concerning the time of the tides. It is a very important clue.

"Court is adjourned."

17

Back in Mason's office, Paul Drake, speaking with his characteristic drawl, said, "I have to hand it to you, Perry. You certainly do pull rabbits out of the hat. You've got the D.A. running around in circles, and the newspapers will give your clients all the best of it when they report this afternoon's session of Court."

"I haven't gotten any rabbits out of any hats yet," Mason said, starting to pace the floor, his thumbs hooked in the armholes of his vest, his head slightly tilted forward so that his eyes seemed to be staring holes in the carpet. 'Hang it, Paul. I'm *almost* in the clear, but I'm afraid I can't go the rest of the way.—I'm glad Judge Newark got the point about the candle and the tides."

"Strange that candle business had never occurred to me," Drake said.

"The explanation's simple," Mason pointed out. "Nearly all murder cases are committed on land. Police detectives get accustomed to thinking in terms of cases on land, and they simply overlook the elemental factors that would automatically enter into the calculations of a yachtsman. Ask a yachtsman about any problem in connection with the ocean, or with navigation, and almost his first thought is about the tide. On the other hand, Lieutenant Tragg and the boys from Homicide probably never think about the tide—unless they happen to be fishermen."

185

"But," Della Street said, "I can't understand how this candle can tie in with . . ."

"With what?" Mason asked.

"With that bloody footprint on the stair tread, or I guess they call it a companionway, using yachting terms, don't they?"

"A companionway is right," Mason said. "And that bloody footprint is the thing that bothers me."

"Carol Burbank made it?"

"She must have. She says she did, and the blood was found on her shoe."

"And there's something wrong with it?" Drake asked.

"The thing that's wrong with it," Mason said, "is that if her story is correct she must have left that bloody footprint *before* the man was murdered."

"But she couldn't have done that, Perry."

"Did you notice the position of that bloody footprint?"

Drake slid around in the big, overstuffed leather chair, said, "Let me take a look at that photograph again, Perry."

Mason opened the drawer in his desk and handed Drake a photograph that showed the print of the bloody foot on the tread of the companionway.

"Well, what's wrong with it?" Drake asked after he'd studied it for some time.

"It wasn't made under the conditions mentioned."

"Why?"

Mason said, "We'll get back to the question of tides again. What's the location of that footprint?"

"Right slap bang in the middle of the tread," Drake said.

"Exactly. Now suppose that at the time she went out there the yacht was heeled way over. She'd have stepped in a pool of blood—then what would have happened? She'd have started up those stairs or, as they call it in yachting terms, companionway. What would have happened? Ever try to climb a slanting stairway?"

"No," Drake said. "Why should I?"

Mason walked over to the closet, took out a stepladder, tilted it very carefully until he was holding it at a certain angle.

"All right," he said, "this is just about the angle of the candle. Now suppose you were going to climb up there. What would you do, Paul?"

Drake said, "If I had to climb up that, I wouldn't."

"Yes you would," Mason told him. "You'd climb up, but what would you do?"

Drake shook his head. "I don't get you."

Della Street walked over to the stepladder, raised her skirts slightly so the men could see the position of her feet clearly. "There's only one way to do it, Paul. You wouldn't put your feet in the center of the treads at all. You'd put them over in the corner, over against the edge of the ladder on the low side."

"Exactly," Mason said.

Drake whistled. "Then you don't think . . ."

"I know," Mason said, "that bloody footprint must have been made when the yacht was on a relatively even keel."

"Well, that's all right, Perry. She *says* she went out there as soon as she got the news. The location of that footprint corroborates her story. The yacht didn't start tilting until around nine o'clock. And Cameron tells about the dinghy being taken out . . ."

"Okay," Mason interrupted, "all that checks. The only trouble with it is that the man wasn't dead then."

"Sure he was. Reconstruct what happened and it all checks. Burbank went out to the yacht with Milfield, had a fight, knocked him over so that the guy's head was cracked on the brass threshold and . . ."

"*Or,*" Mason interrupted, "hit him, knocked him over, cast his rowboat adrift and then came ashore. Someone else rowed out to the yacht, killed Milfield and left. That's what I've got to establish if I'm going to get

187

Burbank and Carol out of this mess. And it's what must have happened."

"Well," Drake said dubiously, "it would be a swell out for you—if you could prove it, Perry. But how can you prove it? There would then have been just two men on the yacht, Milfield and the murderer. Milfield can't talk, and the murderer won't."

Mason said, "Perhaps the murderer will talk. Perhaps he has. And the yacht will talk. All you need to do is to take into consideration the state of the tides, as any yachtsman would do, and you find the story of the prosecution and the story that has been told by the various people simply don't check."

"What does check?" Della Street asked.

Mason resumed his pacing the floor. "This chap, Burwell," he said abruptly, "he seems to be a naïve lad in the throes of a first illicit love affair—but notice that he isn't as naïve as he pretends. He *says* he was coming down here on the Lark, Friday night. Was he? Do you notice that he says Daphne Milfield told *him* of her husband's death *before* Lieutenant Tragg could possibly have told her? Before I visited her. Do you notice how closely the mysterious person who was so interested in the nocturnal habits of sharks resembles this chap, Burwell?

"Let's suppose Roger Burbank hit Milfield and knocked him over. He left in a rage. Carol returns and finds the man lying with his head resting on that brass-covered threshold. She thinks her father must have killed him. Her father thinks so too. But suppose her father didn't kill him? Then we must look to the yacht itself and to the evidence of circumstances to tell us what happened and who *did* kill Milfield. It's simply a matter of trying to get things to check. The elements of the case are so simple that a child can grasp them, but when you put them together, they simply don't fit. Let's look at it from this angle. High tide was at five-forty-one p. m. Take the testimony of the witness, Cameron. Here, I'll make you a schedule."

Mason took a pad of legal foolscap from the desk, picked up a pencil and tabulated certain figures.

Then he passed the schedule across to Paul Drake, and Della Street came to look over his shoulder.

The schedule read:—

Friday night .... high tide 5:41 p. m.
Low tide .... three minutes past midnight, making it 12:03 Saturday morning.
Next high tide .... 6:26 a. m. Saturday morning.
Therefore, boat was aground—so it couldn't have been moved Friday night 8:00 p. m.
Started tilting .... 9:00 p. m.
Had tilted way over .... 10:30 p. m.
Would, therefore, start tilting back .... 2:00 a. m.
Nearly erect, but still aground .... 3:00 a. m.
Floating again .... 4:00 a. m.
Aground again .... 8:45 a. m. Saturday morning.
Started tilting .... 9:45 a. m. Saturday morning.
Tilted way over .... 11:15 a. m.—at time police arrive.

Drake studied the schedule and nodded. "That seems simple enough," he said.

"All right," Mason announced, taking the pad of legal foolscap once more, "here we have a crude diagram of the interior of the cabin and the position of the body. I'll make two positions. Position number one which shows where the body lay when the head struck against the threshold. And position number two, where the body was found.

"Now bear this in mind, Paul: The tilting of the yacht would roll the body down to position number two. But when the next high tide came along, the body *would never roll back to position number one*. All that would happen would be that the yacht, when it floated on the next high tide, would float on an even keel. But because of the position of the anchors and the direction of the tidal currents, when the yacht started to tilt again, it would tilt over to the right side, leaving the starboard side down and the port side up. Therefore, once the body arrived at position number two, it would remain there

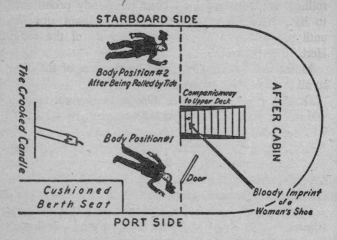

STARBOARD SIDE

Body Position #2
After Being Rolled by Tide

The Crooked Candle

Companionway
to Upper Deck

AFTER CABIN

Body Position #1

Door

Cushioned
Berth Seat

Bloody Imprint
of a
Woman's Shoe

PORT SIDE

until it was moved by some human agency. Here, take a look at the sketch and it will show you what I mean."

Mason handed Drake the sketched diagram.

"Well," Drake said, "there doesn't seem to me to be any great conflict in all of this, Perry."

Mason said, "All right, now let's start checking the testimony and the physical facts of the case with this schedule. The autopsy surgeon says that there were no wounds on the body from which there would have been any bleeding save that gash in the back of the head which was immediately over the fractured portion of the skull and which we may, therefore, refer to as the fatal wound. Now then, there is blood on the threshold at position number one—rather a considerable amount of blood. Here, I'll sketch that in the diagram. There is also some blood near the head of the body in position number two, leaving two distinct pools of blood in the carpet with

190

no connection between them save a few isolated drops of blood which would have been deposited when the body rolled. Now that is to be expected because the body would lie in position number one until the tilting of the yacht caused it to start rolling. But once it had started rolling, the tilt would have been sufficiently pronounced to have made it roll over and over without stopping, until it fetched up against the right side of the cabin. Here, let's check it on the diagram."

Mason put the diagram down on the arm of the chair so all three of them could see it.

Drake studied the diagram silently for several seconds and said, "Well, what's wrong with all that, Perry? That's just the way a body would act. It would lie in one position until the tilt became enough to move it and then when that happened, the body once in motion would roll over and over until it banged up against the low side of the cabin in the position in which it was found."

"Very good," Mason said. "Now notice that the boat started to tilt at nine o'clock Friday night. It hadn't assumed its position of maximum tilt till about ten-thirty p. m. Friday night. Now the candle is tilted at about seventeen degrees, which indicates that at the time it was burning, the yacht had tilted over about half way. Therefore, we might strike some sort of an average—depending on certain factors which we can't anticipate at the present time. But I would be inclined to say that we'd find that intermediate period when the yacht had tilted at about seventeen degrees to be rather shortly after nine o'clock— say around nine-twenty and probably not after nine-thirty, and certainly not after nine-forty.

"Now we start putting things together, bearing in mind the statement of the autopsy surgeon that the period of bleeding did not, in his opinion, cover more than half an hour.

"The body was lying with the head against the threshold of the forward cabin, or within an inch or two of

191

that threshold in what we have referred to in the diagram as position number one, and then it rolled over to position number two, and if the bleeding didn't continue for over half an hour, and if we find blood pools at both position number one and position number two, then we are forced to the conclusion that the murder took place somewhere around nine-fifteen Friday night after the boat had started to tilt."

Drake nodded and said, "That's corroborated by the candle."

"Exactly," Mason said. "The condition of the candle indicates that it burned for about twenty minutes, sometime between nine o'clock p. m. and nine-forty p. m. Probably the candle was lit about nine-twenty and extinguished about nine-forty."

"It was dark before that," Drake said.

"Now you're getting to some of the puzzling features of the case," Mason said. "Either Milfield must have been sitting in the cabin in the dark, or there's another possibility which seems to be much more feasible. That is, that there was an old stub of a candle in the position where the candle was found. Milfield lit that when it got dark, and that candle burnt itself out, whereupon Milfield pried it loose from the board to which it had been stuck, and tossed it overboard. He thereupon lit a fresh candle and . . ."

"By George," Drake said excitedly, "that's it, Perry! That ties the whole thing together. That makes everything check. Milfield had just lit this fresh candle when the murderer came aboard. It must have been within five or ten minutes of the time he lit the candle."

"Exactly," Mason said. "That fixes the time of crime with almost a mathematical certainty, doesn't it, Paul?"

Drake nodded.

"But," Mason said, "Roger Burbank had his altercation with Milfield at around six o'clock in the evening. Carol Burbank drove down to the yacht club as soon as she heard about it. She reached the yacht sometime after seven o'clock and before eight o'clock. The yacht was still on an even keel. She found the body lying in position number one. That's her solemn statement to me."

Drake said, "By George, Perry, you're absolutely right. The girl's lying. She's lying like a trooper about the time element. It simply couldn't have been the way she described it.

"That's right," Mason said. "Everything checks. Carol Burbank is lying. She must have boarded the yacht sometime after nine o'clock. Bear in mind that either the murderer lit the candle, or she lit the candle. There is always the possibility that the candle was lit *after* the murder had been committed, and the murderer had departed."

"Not very likely in view of the fact that the old candle had been removed," Drake said.

"Not very likely," Mason admitted, "but it's a possibility."

Drake said, "You've got me sold, Perry. Carol Burbank is lying."

"Now wait a minute," Mason said. "We come to the one thing which substantiates Carol's story."

"What's that?"

"The location of the bloody footprint. The footprint is right in the middle of the tread of the companionway. That indicates the yacht was on an even keel when the bloody footprint was made. Now how do you account for that, Mr. Detective?"

Drake scratched his head and said, "Damn it, Perry, I don't. It just doesn't fit into the picture at all."

"There you are," Mason said. "That bloody footprint indicates Carol is telling the truth. On the other hand, the evidence of the candle indicates she's lying. The evidence of the bloodstain indicates she's lying. According to the theory of the tides, the murder simply *couldn't* have been committed before nine o'clock.

"And always remember that whenever you're dealing with a murder case, you must take into consideration certain facts. The murderer will always lie. And certain witnesses will sometimes lie. Therefore, you have to take into consideration the fact that the story *anyone* tells, either on or off the stand, may be false."

"Wouldn't it be possible that this footprint could have been framed?" Della Street asked.

"Now," Mason said, "you're getting to the thought that's in the back of my mind. Suppose a girl who knew something about tides, who's smart enough to think fast in an emergency, realized that, for some reason or other, she wanted it to appear the murder had been committed at a time considerably earlier than had actually been the case. The yacht was tilted at the time she was aboard, but she realized that if she left a bloody footprint *in the exact center* of the tread of the companionway, it would indicate the yacht was on an even keel."

"By George!" Drake exclaimed. "Now you've got something! And Carol is a fast-thinking little number."

Mason said almost musingly, "I can't afford to make any fumbles. I've got to hit the bull's-eye with my first and only shot. The autopsy surgeon says the bleeding— that is the extensive bleeding—occupied a period of probably not over thirty minutes. There are just two big pools of blood, one in position number one, and the other in the position in which the body was found. That indicates a murder right around nine-twenty. The position of the candle indicates a murder right around nine-twenty. That bloody footprint is the one thing that doesn't fit into the picture. Now, I've got to know *why* it doesn't fit into the picture, when it was made, how it was made, and *why* it was made."

"Is there a possibility," Della asked, "that the footprint could have been made the next morning after the boat returned to an even keel?"

"That," Mason said, "is the solution that I keep flirting

with. It's the only thing that could possibly account for all the facts as I see them now."

"The question is, would the blood remain moist that long?" Drake asked.

"I think it would," Mason said, "particularly where the blood had soaked into a carpet. Remember that this carpet on the floor of the cabin is very thick and very heavy. It fits into position and is held there by a series of snaps.

"By examining the circumstantial evidence, we have three clocks fixing the time of the murder with mathematical precision. The first and most important clock is the ebbing and flowing of the tide. The second clock is the candle, at an angle of approximately seventeen degrees from the perpendicular, yet with the wax running down smoothly on both sides, indicating that the candle was approximately erect at the time it was burning."

"What's the third clock?" Drake asked.

"The time during which the wound would bleed, probably not more than half an hour. That is, bleeding to the extent that it would leave blood spots the size found in the carpet. Now then, there's only one way you can synchronize all three of those clocks so that they all point to one time as the time of murder, and the minute you do that, that bloody footprint becomes absolutely out of place."

"Then," Drake said, "the footprint was faked. This business of pulling her gloves out of her purse and letting the parcel checking ticket drop to the floor—that's it, Perry, that's bound to be it. The whole thing is some sort of a frame-up."

"On whom?" Mason asked.

"On . . . Gosh, I don't know, Perry. It seems to be on ourselves more than anyone else."

Mason nodded somewhat glumly. "I've covered all of that in my mind, Paul. The footprint is the one thing that doesn't fit in. It's the thing that's out of alignment with everything. Therefore, we must consider the possibility that the footprint was fabricated deliberately, and as you point out, that business of checking the package containing the shoes and subsequently letting the check flutter to the floor, *may* have been just what it seems. But on the other hand it is more apt to have been part of a deliberately planned campaign to get those shoes into the hands of the police under such circumstances that the evidence of the bloodstained shoe would seem to be even more sinister."

Mason took a tide schedule from his pocket and said, "Well, Paul, tonight we're going to make an experiment."

"Just what are your plans?" Drake asked.

"Tonight," Mason said, "high tide is at nine-forty-two p.m. Low tide will be at two-fifty-four a.m. tomorrow morning. According to the schedule we worked out, the boat should be aground about eleven o'clock tonight. It should start tilting at twelve o'clock. It should have tilted away over by one-thirty. Somewhere around half an hour after midnight is the period I want to study, from then until one-forty-five."

"Where's the boat now?" Drake asked.

"As the representative of the owners of the boat," Mason said, "I've been able to get it released from police custody, and it's in my care. I've instructed Cameron at the yacht club to see that the boat is towed out to exactly the position it occupied the night of the murder, and anchored there. Shortly before midnight, we're going down there and study the action of the tide."

Drake's face showed dismay.

"What's the matter?" Mason asked.

Drake said, "You would have to pick the night when I'm nursing a sore throat, and having aches and pains in every joint."

"You're getting the flu?" Mason asked.

"I think I'm headed that way," Drake admitted, "but I

haven't any fever. I'm just feeling uncomfortable. I wanted to go to a Turkish bath, but if you . . ."

"Forget it," Mason interrupted. "There's not a darn thing you can do. I'm just going to study what happens on that boat, and be in a position to advance a theory to the Court tomorrow morning."

"The judge is certainly interested in that candle business," Drake said.

Mason nodded, "If I can work out a theory that will hold water, I can blow that case out of court tomorrow morning. And if I can't, I'm licked."

Della Street said quietly, "I'm going with you, Chief."

"Nonsense," Mason interrupted. "I just want to go down there and see what happens, and . . ."

"And I'm going with you," she interrupted.

"All right," Mason said with a grin. "Come along."

18

A low, thin mist hung over the midnight waters. Above the mist the stars were pale pin-points.

Mason helped Della Street from the car. Their feet echoed along the boards of the float which led to the caretaker's cabin of the yacht club. The silhouettes of the small pleasure yachts tied to the float seemed ghostly and unreal in the damp chill of the night.

A light glowed in the little cabin at the end of the pier, and as the man who was sitting in the warm interior of the office heard the pound of Mason's heels and the quick staccato *tap tap tap* of Della Street's feet, he opened the door and grinned a greeting.

"Hello, Cameron," Mason said.

"Evenin'," Cameron greeted them.

"Is everything all ready?"

Cameron's eyes twinkled in quiet humor. A short, stubby pipe was gripped in his teeth firmly. He removed this pipe, said, "Better come in for a few minutes and get warm. It's going to be mighty cold out there on the water. There's a stove in the cabin of the yacht, but you'll be plenty cold getting out there. I've got a kettle of hot water on the stove and some rum. If you folks would like a hot buttered rum, I . . ."

Mason didn't even wait for him to finish. "What is holding you back?" he demanded.

Cameron smiled and, glancing at Della Street, asked Mason somewhat diffidently, "Two glasses or three?"

It was Della who answered the question. "Three," she announced.

"And you can make 'em just as strong as you like," Mason said.

Cameron put a generous portion of butter into three cups, adding boiling water, sugar, spices, and then poured in the rum. "Got a brother in the dairy business," he said. "Manage to keep myself supplied with enough butter to take the edge off my rum toddies. You folks want to take your coats off?"

"No," Mason said. "We'll get started as soon as we've finished our rum, and it won't do us any harm to get good and warm before we start."

Della and Mason silently toasted each other over the rims of the thick porcelain cups, then sipped the hot beverage.

"That," Mason announced, "is a lifesaver."

"Uh huh. Kind of crisp tonight. It gets chilly along about midnight down on the water eight or nine months out of the year. I have to get out and make the rounds ever so often. I'm telling you, it certainly feels good to come back to my cozy little cabin."

"Don't you get lonely?" Della asked.

Cameron puffed contentedly on his pipe. "Nope," he said, "I've got books and—well, I don't know. You get lonely in a big house, but in a little cabin like this with everything ship-shape, you don't get lonesome. You get so after a while you can get along with yourself better than with anybody else."

"How long will it take us to get out to the yacht?" Mason asked.

"Oh, not over ten minutes. Now as I get it, you want to have me take you out there with my outboard motor, and leave you there. Then I'm to come back for you around two o'clock. That right?"

"That's right."

"Okay," Cameron said, "I'll be there. Just wanted to

get the time straight in my mind because I hate to leave this place alone. I really ain't supposed to, but I guess a short trip like this won't hurt anything. But I'd like to time things so you'll be ready to start back soon's I get there. You found some clue?"

Mason laughed. "Not a clue. We're just looking around."

"Humph!"

"Of course we *might* find something."

"That's right. How'd I do on the witness stand today? Didn't hurt your case any, did I?"

"Not a bit."

"That's good. I hope you get both of them off. They're fine people. Mr. Burbank is a good friend of mine. And that daughter of his. Say, there's a live wire for you! A regular little thoroughbred, that girl! Well, anytime you're ready to start."

Mason and Della Street placed their empty cups on the drain board of the little sink. "Let's go," Mason said.

The outboard motor sputtered into life. The bow of the boat moving through the water pushed ahead of it a bow wave which broke out into a series of ripples on each side. The cold night air brushed moist, chill fingers against their faces. The little boat chugged out into the channel, then after a minute or two rounded a point and started fighting against the tide up the black waters of the estuary.

"Rather hard to navigate here?" Mason said.

"Oh, you get so you know your way around. Learn a few simple landmarks and you're okay. Keep the tip of that point outlined against that little glow of light on the other side. Keep 'em right in line. See, I've got 'em dead astern."

Mason laughed, "You'll have me applying for a pilot's license directly."

Della Street said, "Something ahead."

The outboard motor promptly slowed its speed.

"That's the yacht," the boatman said.

They swung around the yacht in a circle, came up close to the rail. The boatman said to Mason, "Now if you can just get aboard . . ."

Mason nodded, reached up, caught the cold, clammy, iron handrail of the yacht, and clambered aboard. The boatman tossed him a rope, said to Della, "Now, Miss, I'll give you a hand."

They boosted Della Street up to the deck of the yacht. Cameron moved over to cling to the handrail, holding the skiff up against the yacht. "She's aground already," he said.

"That's right."

"Well, watch your step when she settles. She'll go over part way, then sort of stick and then go way over with a lurch. Now, you want me back here at two o'clock. That right?"

"That's right," Mason said.

"Okay, I'll be here. You watch your step now. Don't get hurt."

"We won't," Mason promised.

Cameron still seemed reluctant to shove off. He continued for several seconds to stand holding the rail, the idling outboard motor pop-pop-popping, a faint odor of burnt gasoline clinging to the water. "Well, I'll be on my way. Right around two o'clock, eh?"

"That's right."

"Think you'll be all done and ready to start back by that time?"

"I think so."

"Well, I'll be seeing you."

Cameron pushed the skiff clear, settled back in the stern. The outboard purred into activity and within a matter of seconds the skiff was lost to sight, although the sound of the motor continued to drift back through the misty darkness.

"Well," Mason said, taking a flashlight from his pocket, "let's go below. Watch your step, Della, the deck's slippery."

Mason took a key from his pocket, unlocked a padlock, slid back the hatch, assisted Della Street down the companionway, and into the main cabin.

"How cozy," Della exclaimed.

"It is, all right," Mason agreed, lighting a candle.

"What did they do for heat?"

"There's a little stove that burns wood and coal," Mason said. "They used it for cooking as well as for heating. I told Cameron I wanted a fire laid in it. Yes, it's all ready to start going."

Mason lit a match, tossed it into the stove. The paper and kindling crackled into cheery flame. Mason said, "Now then, all we have to do is to wait for the tide to run out."

Della Street looked at her wrist watch. "The boat is aground now?"

"Yes," Mason said, "the keel's resting on the mud."

The yacht gave a slight, all but imperceptible list.

"Not only aground," Mason said, "but it's going to start tilting in a few minutes. Well, it won't take us long now. I want to see just exactly how long before low tide a body would roll to the lower side of the cabin, and just how the yacht starts listing as the tide runs out."

Della shivered slightly.

"Getting nervous?" Mason asked.

"A little," she admitted. "It's creepy here. Let's blow out the candle and wait here in the dark. The stove will give out enough light. . . . I feel sort of conspicuous. . . . Anyone could. . . . Well, you know . . . through the porthole. . . ." She broke off and laughed.

Mason promptly blew out the candle.

"There, that's better," Della said. "I had the feeling that eyes were peering through the portholes."

Mason slipped his arm around her, "Forget it," he said. "No one even knows we're out here."

She laughed, a little apologetic laugh, and pressed herself close to his protecting shoulder.

The fire crackled merrily. Little ruddy reflections of flame flickered out from the draft in the front of the stove. Silence descended upon them, a silence broken only by the gurgling sound of tide water swirling past the grounded yacht.

The yacht swung a little more over to the side, moving almost imperceptibly.

Mason consulted the luminous dial of his wrist watch, said, "Well, here's where I lie down on the floor and pretend I'm a dead body."

Della Street glanced over in the direction of the dark red stain on the carpet and said, "I don't like to have you lie there."

"Why?"

"It seems too sinister. It might bring . . . Can't you lie in another part of the yacht just as well?"

"No," Mason said, "I'm going to conduct the experiment right here."

Mason stretched himself out on the carpeted floor of the cabin, his head within a few inches of the brass door sill of the cabin in the rear of the boat.

"Okay, Della?"

"Well, it's sort of creepy. Makes you think of ghosts."

"If Milfield's ghost could only come back and tell us exactly what happened," Mason said, "it would be a break for us."

Della came over to sit on the floor beside him. Her hand slid down Mason's arm, her fingers found his hand, and closed about it.

Mason patted her shoulder, said, "Remember, I'm supposed to be a corpse."

She laughed, "Don't you feel like a corpse?"

"No."

The boat moved sluggishly, taking a little more list.

"Not enough slant as yet to roll me down to the other

side," Mason observed, "—when that happens, we'll take a look at the watch and notice the exact time. Where's the flashlight, Della?"

"On the table."

Mason sighed wearily. "It certainly was quite a day in court. Hard as this floor is, it feels nice and restful."

Della took her hand from his, let her fingertips stroke his forehead, "You should take things easier."

"Uh huh," Mason agreed somewhat drowsily, asked a few minutes later, "What time is it now, Della?"

She looked at his wrist watch. "Getting along toward one-thirty."

"Another ten or fifteen minutes should tell the story," Mason observed.

Abruptly Della Street shifted her position. "You don't need to be so darned uncomfortable," she said. "Here, lift up your head."

She placed his head on her lap. "There, that's better. Now, you can tell just as much about it as you can with your head lying on that hard floor."

"I can't," Mason protested drowsily. "I should have my head down there . . . on the floor. . . . I want to know the exact time. . . . Oh well . . . perhaps this will do if I keep completely relaxed."

Her fingers moved along his forehead, the fingertips caressed his eyebrows and the closed eyes, smoothed back his hair.

"You just lie there and relax," she said softly.

Mason raised his hand to hers, moved it to his lips, held it there for a moment, then released it.

A moment later, his regular breathing showed that he was asleep, and, in his sleep, his hand once more groped for Della's, held it close.

Minutes passed with no change in the situation. Della Street sat motionless. The boat, firmly aground now, seemed to have ceased tilting.

Della Street herself became drowsy. The warmth of the

cabin, the utter quiet which enveloped them, the relaxing of taut nerves after a hard day in court, coupled with the lateness of the hour, made her head nod in little snatches of welcome sleep.

Abruptly the cabin floor gave a peculiar lurch. The yacht hesitated for a moment, then suddenly heeled way over.

For the moment, Della Street, startled to wakefulness, was too frightened to say anything. She grasped instinctively at the doorway of the cabin for support. Perry Mason's limp body rolled over and over. The lawyer, wakened from a sound sleep, clawed at the carpet in a sudden automatic reflex action. Then Della heard a thud as Mason banged up against the starboard wall of the cabin.

A moment later, she heard his laugh from the darkness. "Well, Della, I guess I went to sleep and that did it. The time seems to be exactly one-forty-three. According to my mental arithmetic, that's almost exactly four hours and one minute after high tide. Of course, there's a slight difference in the height of the tides which we'll have to take into consideration, but it's only a few inches and . . ."

"What's that?" Della Street asked, startled, as Mason abruptly stopped talking.

"Listen!" he cautioned.

They listened. From the outer darkness came a peculiar rhythmic thumping sound which grew momentarily louder—a sound which had a peculiar jarring undertone that seemed to strike the hull of the boat with a distinct impact.

"What is it?" Della Street whispered.

"A rowboat," Mason announced in a low voice.

"Coming this way?"

"Yes."

"Do you suppose it's the man coming back for us?— Perhaps his outboard motor went wrong and . . ."

"Too early," Mason said. "Keep quiet, Della. Where are you?"

"Over here by the stove, getting the poker," she said. "If this should be the murderer . . . !"

"Hush," Mason warned.

He groped toward her in the darkness, whispered, "Let's find that flashlight."

"I've been looking for it," she whispered. "When the boat heeled over, it must have rolled off the table. Here, Chief, you take this poker. It's heavy and . . ."

Abruptly the jarring impact ran through the yacht as a rowboat thudded against the side of the yacht's hull.

Heavy feet pounded on the deck above them. The hatchway made noise as it slid back along the metallic guides.

Mason pulled Della Street toward the doorway leading to the rear cabin. "Quick," he said in a whisper, "in the cabin!"

As Mason pushed Della Street into the rear cabin, a flashlight sent a brilliant circle of light down into the cabin, then was promptly extinguished. A leg swung over to the companionway and stopped. For a few seconds the intruder was motionless, then the leg was withdrawn. The hatch slammed back into position. Steps made sound across the sloping deck, thudded into the rowboat. Oars made a frantic splashing.

"Quick," Mason said, groping toward the companionway, "get that flashlight, Della. Feel along on the low side of the cabin. It will have rolled down there. Get it and give it to me."

Mason pushed up the companionway, thrust his head and shoulders out into the chill of the night air.

The mist had settled into a damp fog which hung over the water like a fleece, blanketing sounds, distorting perspective.

Panic-stricken oars were splashing vigorously out in the milky darkness.

"Hey, you," Mason called, "come back here!"

The frenzied speed of the oars was redoubled, but no other answer came from the fog-filled darkness.

"Here's the light, Chief."

Della thrust the metallic cylinder into the lawyer's hand. He pressed the button, sent a beam of light out into the fog. It was no more effective then if the beam had tried to penetrate watered milk.

The sound of oars was growing momentarily fainter.

Mason muttered his impatience.

"What frightened him?" Della asked. "We didn't make any noise."

"The stove," Mason explained. "He slid back the hatch above the companionway and the heat came rushing up to meet him. He knew then someone was aboard."

"Gosh, Chief, I was so scared! My joints are all jelly— particularly my knees."

Mason drew her to him. He switched off the flashlight, stood with Della pressed close, listening.

There was a faint dripping sound as fog condensations dropped from the yacht. Otherwise, there was no sound.

"He may have quit rowing and is letting the tide take him out," Mason said, disappointment in his voice. "Lord, how I wish Cameron would show up with that outboard!"

They stood straining their ears, then Della stirred uneasily, "Chief, I think I hear it!"

Once more they listened. A peculiar undertone of sound grew in volume, became unmistakably the staccato of an outboard motor.

"He's coming from the direction where that rowboat disappeared," Mason said. "He may run right on it. Let's get him to hurry."

He snapped the flashlight, elevated the beam, swung it in a series of circles, signaling the boat into greater speed.

Within a minute or two, the skiff came gliding toward them out of the darkness, the outboard motor ceasing its pulsations as an expert hand guided the skiff up to the low side of the yacht.

"Come on, Della," Mason said. "Let's go."

Bracing himself, he placed his hands beneath her shoulders and swung her clear of the deck and into the skiff. A moment later, Mason was in beside her.

"Quick," he said to Cameron. "There's a rowboat we want to catch. It's back in the direction you came from. Give it all you've got for about two minutes, then shut off the motor and we'll listen."

"A rowboat?" the boatman asked. "I haven't rented any boats. I . . ."

"Never mind," Mason said, "let's get started."

The outboard motor roared into action once more. Water churned up in the rear of the skiff and as the little craft gathered headway, the moisture-beaded air struck against the faces of the passengers.

"All right," Mason said after a couple of minutes. "Let's stop and listen."

Cameron shut off the motor. The boat glided along through the water, the gurgling sound which accompanied its motion for the moment making it impossible to hear anything else. Then gradually as the boat lost momentum, the silence gripped them—a fog-filled silence broken only by a very faint lapping of water against the bow of the boat. There were no sounds of oars in oarlocks.

After two or three minutes of tense listening, Cameron said, "You can't do anything this way unless you happen to run right on him. He'll hear you coming, get out of the way, quit rowing when you shut off the motor and then start rowing again when he hears the motor."

"All right, then," Mason said. "There's only one thing to do. That's zigzag back and forth. He must be around here somewhere."

Immediately Cameron started the motor. The little skiff zigzagged back and forth through the fog. Mason sat up in the bow, his face straining through the darkness, searching for the vague indistinct shape on the water that he hoped would glide by, or, perhaps, loom up directly in front of the skiff.

He saw nothing.

Once more the motor slowed to almost silence. Cameron called out, "I don't dare to do any more, Mr. Mason. I'm going to get lost. You can't see your landmarks here. I'm not too certain where I am right now."

"All right," Mason conceded. "I guess it's like looking for a needle in a haystack. Which way is the yacht? I want to go back again."

"Well," the boatman conceded, "I'm not just exactly certain, but I'll see if I can find it. It should be around here."

He swung the bow of the skiff, held it steady. "I can't leave my place there for too long a time," he said. "I'm really not supposed to leave at all. What would anyone want aboard that yacht?"

Mason said, "I'm beginning to wonder about that myself. He'd hardly have been trying to remove something. Perhaps he knew we were aboard—Say, wait a minute. Perhaps we don't want to go back to that yacht. He may have been . . ."

Off to the right and perhaps a quarter of a mile ahead, a sheet of flame mushroomed into an exploding pattern that ripped apart the night with a concussion that all but knocked them flat in the boat. A half moment later, the roar of sound crashed against their eardrums.

Instinctively the boatman shut off the motor. The boat drifted for a moment in a silence that seemed as a tangible wall blocking all sensation from their eardrums.

High overhead, there was a whirring sound in the air—a sound which grew in intensity and was followed by a splash some hundred yards off to the left. A moment later, other splashes sounded all around them.

"Falling debris," Mason said.

Cameron shifted his pipe in his mouth. "That there

explosion," he said, "must have been what you was thinking of when you changed your mind about going back."

"And that's that," Mason said grimly. "Let's get back."

The outboard motor snarled into high speed. The little skiff fairly leaped ahead in the water then swung in a wide half circle. The particles of fog moisture misted against the faces of the passengers until the fog seemed to have turned to a drizzling rain. The cold damp chill which lay along the water penetrated through their garments to the very bone.

"Won't be long," Cameron said. "Just hope I'm not lost, that's all."

There followed an interval of several minutes during which the three persons in the little boat were too chilled and uncomfortable to do any talking. Then a sparbuoy loomed up out of the darkness almost dead ahead. Cameron swung the skiff so as to just miss the buoy, then after a few moments, swung the boat hard to port. A vague shadowy mass of land loomed against pale stars as the fog suddenly thinned. A light appeared ahead with a halo of moisture surrounding it. The little skiff swept around in a curve and, seemingly without warning, the darkness ahead resolved itself into mist-enshrouded outlines of yachts moored to the float at the yacht club.

Even in the short time that the journey had consumed, the cold had cramped Mason's limbs, and it was with an effort that he jumped to the float, carrying the painter.

Cameron shut off the motor, took the painter from Mason and tied it to a ring in the float. "How you coming?" he asked Della Street.

"B-r-r-r!" she said and laughed.

The three of them walked down the float and Cameron opened the door of his snug little cabin. The welcome warmth from the stove enveloped them with a silent hospitality. The singing teakettle was as homelike as the purring of a cat in front of a fireplace.

Without a word, Cameron switched on the lights,

poured hot water over spices, butter and sugar, in three cups, and added lots of rum.

"This," Mason announced, "hits the spot."

"This," Della Street supplemented, "is saving my life. I thought I wouldn't make it. Clothes don't seem to be any good at all against that cold fog."

Cameron lit his pipe. "Goes right through you," he admitted.

He raised the lid of the stove, thrust in two sticks of heavy oak, and was refilling the teakettle when he paused, his eyes peering out through the window.

"Car coming."

"What time is it?" Mason asked.

"Two-fifteen."

"Seems like it's been ages," Della Street laughed.

Mason took pencil and paper from his pocket. "I want to look at your tide table," he said. "I want to find out just how much difference there was between the tide tonight and the night of the murder. I . . ."

"Coming this way," Cameron reported. "A couple of men. Look like officers."

Feet pounded along the float with a strange booming note.

"Sounds like a drum," Della Street said, and coughed nervously, "an ominous drum."

Two men opened the door of the cabin without knocking. For the moment, they ignored Mason and Della Street, their eyes fastened on Cameron. "What was that explosion?" they asked.

"Burbank's yacht blew up."

"That's what we thought. You take anyone out there tonight?"

Cameron gestured toward Perry Mason and Della Street.

"You can swear they were aboard the yacht?"

"That's right."

211

"How long after they left did the explosion take place?"

"Between five and ten minutes. Not over ten minutes."

The officer regarded Mason with square-jawed belligerency. "Get your things, buddy. You're going to Headquarters."

"Don't be silly," Mason told him. "I've got to be in court tomorrow. I'm Perry Mason."

"I don't give a damn if you're Pontius Pilate, you're going to Headquarters."

Mason explained patiently, "There was a rowboat that came out to the yacht. I thought at the time it was someone who wanted to get something that was on the yacht, but that he became frightened when he opened the hatch and found there was a fire going in the cabin stove. I realize now that what he wanted was to plant a time bomb. He didn't know just how soon we were leaving the yacht, and thought that was a good chance to blow up both us and the yacht. That business of opening the hatch and starting down to the cabin, then turning and running from the yacht and rowing frantically away into the darkness was just part of the stall to keep us from getting suspicious as to what he had really been after. He probably planted the bomb within a matter of seconds after getting aboard the yacht."

"What did this man look like?"

"We didn't see him."

"What sort of a boat?"

"We didn't see that."

The officer grinned—a tantalizing, superior grin. "You've got to do better than that," he said, and then added reproachfully, "And you a lawyer, too."

Mason said, "For the love of Mike! Get Headquarters on your radio. Have them cover the entire waterfront. Try and pick up anyone who's prowling around. See if you can't locate that rowboat when the man comes ashore—if he hasn't landed already."

"And make a monkey out of myself falling for a story like that and turning the department upside down. No, Mason, I'm sorry, but as far as we're concerned, you're elected. You and this lady went out to the yacht. What did you go out there for?"

"To study the action of the tides."

"Nice stuff," the officer said sarcastically. "You carry along a time bomb. You wait until just when you're leaving and then press the button and start the thing going. You've timed it so you can get clean away."

"Don't be silly," Mason said. "Why would I want to blow up the yacht?"

"Why would anybody want to blow up the yacht? You've got more reason than anyone." The officer turned to Cameron. "Did he come straight back, or did he make some excuse to hang around somewhere near the yacht until the thing blew up?"

Cameron hesitated.

"Go ahead," the officer said.

"It wasn't that," Cameron finally blurted. "We were looking around in the fog for this rowboat, zigzagging back and forth."

"Somewheres near the yacht?"

"About quarter of a mile."

The officer exchanged glances with his companion, then sniffed audibly and looked at the empty cups. "What you got there," he asked Cameron, "rum?"

"We did have," Cameron said dryly, filling his pipe and making no move toward the rum bottle.

The officer jerked his head at Perry Mason. "Okay," he said, "come along—you and the lady, both."

19

The light in the branch police station consisted of a single electric globe screwed into a porcelain reflector in the ceiling. It was a harsh, trying light that beat down upon tired eyes, yet furnished an insufficient illumination to show objects in the room clearly.

Perry Mason, his face bearing traces of strain and weariness, tilted back in his chair, put his feet on the corner of the battered table and looked at his watch. "Damn it," he said, "*I* can take it. But *you're* going to get some sleep, Della."

She said, "There doesn't seem to be anything we can do."

"We'll give them five minutes more and then we're going to do plenty," Mason said. "I . . ."

The door opened. The officer who had taken Mason into custody stood to one side while Lieutenant Tragg entered the room, then followed the Lieutenant in and closed the door.

"Now then," the officer said, "suppose you tell the Lieutenant what actually happened. You . . ."

"I'll do the talking, Medford," Lieutenant Tragg interrupted, and turning to Mason asked, "What happened?"

Mason nodded toward the officer whom Tragg had addressed as Medford. "Your skeptical friend let the murderer slip through his fingers."

"Tell me about it," Tragg invited.

Mason told about going to the yacht, about the visit of the rowboat and the explosion.

"What did you want aboard the yacht?" Tragg asked.

Mason said frankly, "I wanted to study the effects of the tide."

"What about it?"

"I wanted to lie flat on the floor and see just how long after high tide the boat took enough of a tilt so I'd roll down to the lower side of the cabin."

"What did you find out?" Tragg asked, his voice showing his interest.

"Four hours and one minute after high tide the yacht settled over enough so I rolled down to the starboard side."

"How long after high tide?" Tragg asked incredulously.

"Four hours and one minute exactly," Mason repeated and yawned. "It will be necessary to co-ordinate that time with the tidal differences in feet and inches. And now, my dear Lieutenant, Della Street and I are either going home, or someone's going to have to swear out a warrant for us. Make up your mind."

Tragg said, "That's all, Medford. You may go now."

The officer hesitated. "You could tell they were guilty the way they acted, Lieutenant. I wish you could have seen their faces when I picked them up."

"I wish I could have. But that's all, Medford."

Reluctantly, Medford left the room.

Tragg turned to Mason, said thoughtfully, "That would make the time of the murder right around nine-forty."

"Subject to adjustments," Mason amended. "But remember the prosecution fixes the time at around five-thirty or six o'clock."

"No more it doesn't," Tragg admitted promptly, "not after the stuff you brought out about the tide and what the doctor testified to about hemorrhage."

"I'm afraid Hamilton Burger doesn't agree with you."

"I wouldn't want to be quoted on that, but I *could* tell you something."

"What?"

"Judge Newark agrees with you. The judge is going to do a little arithmetic in court tomorrow—I'm not violating any confidence when I'm telling you that your friend, Hamilton Burger, is a badly puzzled man. You should have heard him interviewing Douglas Burwell."

"Oh, you found *him,* did you?" Mason asked.

"Sure we found him."

"What did he say?"

"That story about coming down Friday night on the Lark was the bunk. He came down on a plane Friday afternoon. Mrs. Milfield telephoned him that she'd intended to run away with him, but after getting as far as the airport, she'd decided it never would work and she was going back home. He rushed to the airport, managed to get a canceled plane reservation and flew down to Los Angeles to talk with her. They talked for a while. Daphne Milfield was terribly nervous. She finally said her husband was aboard Burbank's yacht, and that she'd talk with her husband; that she wasn't going to just sneak away. She suggested that Burwell go down to the yacht club, rent a rowboat and then pick her up down at the point. There's a litte rickety landing down there."

"Why didn't she go with him to rent the boat?" Mason asked.

"She told him that the man at the yacht club knew her and she didn't want to be seen with Burwell."

"Go on, let's hear the rest of it."

"He rowed down to the point. Mrs. Milfield was there on the landing. He isn't much of a hand with a boat. She's an expert. She rowed him out to the yacht, left him in the rowboat, went aboard, lit a candle and stayed aboard for some twenty minutes while her shivering boy friend hung around the rowboat. The yacht was then heeled pretty well over. Burwell didn't hear any voices.

He didn't hear any struggle. Mrs. Milfield came back and told him that she thought things were going to be all right; that her husband was going to make a sensible property settlement and she'd be free to leave as soon as the papers were drawn up. Burwell was to go to the hotel and wait."

"Did Burwell ask any questions?"

"Don't be silly. The guy's in love. He swallowed everything she told him. Along about eleven o'clock the next morning, Mrs. Milfield rang him up and told him her husband was dead; that Burwell was to swear he came down on the Lark and had arrived that morning; that he wasn't, under any circumstances, to try and see her or to mention anything about the trip to the yacht."

"What does Mrs. Milfield say?" Mason asked.

"Mrs. Milfield breaks down with a complete admission. She says Burwell is telling the truth; that she went out to the yacht to see her husband; that when she got out there, she found him lying on the floor dead."

"Where?" Mason asked.

"That," Tragg said, "is the point. She says he was lying on the port side of the yacht with his head within an inch or two of the brass-covered threshold. She says the yacht had begun to tilt, but hadn't tilted way over; that you could walk around in it all right by hanging onto things; that a candle had been left on the table and had burned itself completely out. There was nothing left but a blob of wax. She says the wax was still warm and soft. She lit a fresh candle and stuck it in the wax. She put it in so that it was straight up and down. She says she softened up the wax just a little with the flame of the candle and then put this fresh candle in the pool of wax. She's frank enough to admit that her husband didn't mean a damn thing to her except by way of being a meal ticket. He had an interest in these oil properties and she decided it would be poor business to walk out on him just before he became a millionaire. She decided she wanted a property settlement. When she saw she was going to be a rich widow, she thought she'd like to play it that way."

"Why does she say she changed her mind about going to San Francisco?"

"A friend of her husband caught up with her, told her it wouldn't work. She knew he was right. She'd have ducked out on the whole business then—if Burwell hadn't hopped a plane and flown down."

"How does Burger feel about all this?" Mason asked.

"Burger feels like hell," Tragg said. "He wouldn't like it if he knew I'd told you all this. I'm telling you for one reason."

"What's the reason?" Mason asked.

"So you can tell me what's on *your* mind and then sleep late in the morning."

Mason laughed. "I'll sleep late anyway. I won't even go near the damn court. I'll send Jackson down. I know darn well Burger will be yelling for a continuance."

Tragg puffed at his cigar. "You're a tough customer, Mason."

"I'm not naturally tough. I've learned to be tough through rubbing elbows with the police. I don't know why I should give you anything, Tragg. You're always trying to hit back at me, and this time you tried to hit back through Della."

"Because you led with Della," Tragg replied. "You and I are on opposite sides of the fence, Mason. Your methods are brilliant enough, but they aren't regular. As long as you play the game the way you do, I'm going to crack down on you every chance I get. Only this time, I'm holding out an olive branch. You give me your ideas and we'll forget about Della Street and those bloodstained shoes."

Mason gave the proposition thoughtful consideration "I'll go this far with you, Tragg, but only this far. I'll give you the key clue to the whole business."

"What's the key clue?"

"A person climbing a *tilted* companionway would leave a bloody footprint on the low side—not in the center."

Tragg's forehead creased into a frown. "What the devil are you talking about?"

"I'm giving you the key clue, the most significant fact in the entire case."

Tragg chewed on his cigar. "Hang it, Mason, you may be getting Roger Burbank out of the frying pan by getting Carol Burbank into the fire."

Mason said, "I'm just giving you the key clue; you can figure it out. Take a stepladder, tilt it over at an angle and experiment. A person climbing a companionway would only put a foot in the middle of the tread when the yacht was on an even keel. If the yacht were tilted, the print would be way over on the low side of the tread. Try it with a stepladder. We did."

Tragg smoked silently. Abruptly he said, "I guess you've talked too damn much, Mason. I'm taking back my olive branch."

Mason yawned, ground out the end of his cigarette. "The reason I'm not going all the way with you, Tragg, is because you tried to pick on Della. I didn't like that."

"I don't give a damn whether you like it or not. You use her to pull chestnuts out of the fire for you, my lad, and we'll burn her fingers for her. . . . And don't be too certain you're in the clear on blowing up that boat to conceal the evidence, wise guy."

"What evidence?" Mason asked.

"The exact time it would tilt over far enough so a body would roll down to the low side of the cabin."

"I've told you what I found out," Mason said.

"Yes, so you have—the uncorroborated word of the lawyer who is representing the owner of the bloodstained shoe."

"Don't you believe me?"

"I don't know. A jury sure as hell wouldn't."

219

Mason smiled. "I think they would, Lieutenant. Come on, Della. Let's go."

A surprised Medford watched them emerge from the room, gazed after them with silent hostility as Mason piloted Della Street down the corridor.

"*Good* morning, officer," Mason said. "I rather think Tragg wants to talk with you."

20

Judge Newark, taking his place on the bench, glanced inquiringly down at the vacant counsel seat beside Jackson. "Mr. Mason is not here?" he asked.

"Mr. Mason has asked me to carry on for the defense," Jackson announced with dignity.

"If the Court please," Maurice Linton began, "the prosecution wishes to . . ."

"Just a moment," Judge Newark interposed. "The Court wishes to make an announcement before anything further is said by counsel on either side. The Court will take judicial cognizance of the tide tables, but it is possible that there is some difference in the time of tides at the particular spot where the yacht was anchored. I am inclined to believe the extent of the estuary—the body of water which is behind a certain given point and which, I believe, has a certain inertia, constitutes a local variation. The Court would like to receive evidence of the exact time lag between the published time schedules and the point where the yacht was anchored at the time of the murder. Is it possible to introduce such evidence at this time without seriously disrupting your plan of presentation, Mr. District Attorney?"

Hamilton Burger arose with slow and ponderous dignity. "I am afraid, if the Court please, that is hardly possible. The overnight developments in this case have been such that the prosecution wishes to ask for a continuance. I feel that I am not out of order in disclosing to the Court that the yacht was destroyed last night by what appears to have been a time bomb."

Judge Newark cleared his throat. "Did the prosecution make any experiments prior to the destruction of this yacht?"

"I am sorry to say we did not, Your Honor. I understand experiments were conducted by Mr. Mason."

"And Mr. Mason is not here?"

"No, Your Honor."

Judge Newark picked up a pencil. "The Court has taken a deep interest in this matter of the tides. The entire case may hinge upon them. What is your attitude in regard to a continuance, Mr. Jackson?"

"I have been instructed to oppose it," Jackson said.

"I believe," Judge Newark observed, "there is a code provision limiting continuances to no more than two days at a time, or more than six days in all, and motions for continuance must be made upon affidavit. Do you have an affidavit, Mr. Burger?"

"No, Your Honor. I really feel that it would not be at all to the detriment of these defendants to consent to a continuance."

"Counsel for the defendants seem to feel otherwise."

"If the matter could be postponed until this afternoon," Hamilton Burger pleaded desperately, "I think that I could get in touch with Mr. Mason personally, and . . ."

"What's your attitude in regard to a continuance until this afternoon?" Judge Newark asked Jackson.

"I've been instructed to oppose *all* continuances, Your Honor."

"Very well, the prosecution will proceed with its case."

Hamilton Burger announced with dignity, "Under those circumstances, Your Honor, the prosecution asks that the case be dismissed."

Judge Newark's face darkened. "Of course Counsel

has it in his power to thwart the wishes of the Court. Inasmuch as jeopardy does not attach until . . ."

Judge Newark hesitated as though wondering just how strong to carry his rebuke.

Jackson interpolated, "I have been instructed not to oppose a dismissal, Your Honor."

Judge Newark reached his decision. "Very well, the case is dismissed. The defendants are discharged from custody. I deem it only fair, however, to state that in the event the defendants are arrrested again, the Court will take into consideration what has happened in this matter. Court is adjourned."

Judge Newark arose from the bench, started for his chambers, then turned and said, "May I ask Counsel for both sides to appear in Chambers?"

Jackson hurried to a phone booth in the corridor, dialed Mason's office and said imploringly, "Gertie, is the boss around?"

"He hasn't come in yet."

"There's a mess down here. The judge has asked Counsel to meet with him in Chambers. I don't like it. He's become all worked up over some theory of tides. I think Mr. Mason should be here."

"What did they do with the case?"

"Dismissed it."

"Okay. I'll try and get the boss. You stall things along. I'll have Mr. Mason telephone if he comes in. That may mollify the old bird."

"It is hardly seeming to refer to Judge Newark in such a manner," Jackson reproached with supercilious dignity.

"He's an old bird as far as I'm concerned," Gertie said cheerfully, and hung up.

Jackson crossed the courtroom and opened the door of Judge Newark's chambers.

Hamilton Burger and Maurice Linton seemed somewhat ill at ease. Judge Newark was writing down figures on a scratch pad. He glanced up, said, "Come in, Mr. Jackson. Where's Mason?"

"He hasn't showed up at the office yet. I've left word for him to call."

"Very well," Judge Newark said. "Sit down. Gentlemen, I am fully aware that under the law as it now exists, you can short-circuit a committing magistrate altogether. However, I don't like those tactics."

Burger said apologetically, "I didn't want to make the announcement publicly, Judge, but Mrs. Milfield now admits she was aboard that yacht about nine-thirty Friday night. A young man with whom she appears to be infatuated rented a rowboat from Cameron and took her out to that yacht."

Judge Newark noted the time on the sheet of foolscap, made some more figures and pursed his lips.

"Does she claim her husband was alive then?"

"She claims he was dead. She claims she found him lying in what Counsel for the defense has referred to as position number one—the head near the brass-covered threshold leading to the stateroom."

"Why didn't she report it?" Judge Newark asked.

"Afraid that she'd be accused of murdering him. She tried to cover up."

"Humph!"

"That's exactly the way I felt about it," Burger said.

Judge Newark began drawing aimless lines on the pad of legal paper. "The doctor's testimony is that there wouldn't have been an active hemorrhage for more than a period of some twenty minutes after the fatal blow had been struck. Therefore, the murder *must* have been committed at a time when the yacht had begun to tilt, but hadn't as yet assumed its maximum tilt. Its tilt or list, however, must have increased within a period of twenty minutes after the crime so that the body rolled over to the low side of the yacht. Now the question is, how does that list take place? Is it a slow, gradual list, or does the boat tilt part way over, remain in that position for a while and then make a last sudden shift of position? That's the important question in this case. Can you answer it?"

"I can't," Hamilton Burger admitted.

"That's the important point in the case," the judge said, his voice containing a rebuke.

"I know it," Burger admitted, and then added ruefully, "Now ..."

The door of the chambers opened and Perry Mason, buoyant and well-groomed, bowed and said, "Good morning, gentlemen."

Judge Newark's face showed relief. "Mr. Mason," he said, "I have become very much interested in this question of tides. I think it's going to be possible to solve the case by taking them into consideration. Will you tell me what you discovered last night? You seem to be the only one who realized the importance of getting this information."

Mason grinned. "The boat seems to rest on the ground about two hours and fifteen or twenty minutes after high tide. It tilts more or less gradually until it reaches an angle of around seventeen degrees. Then there is a quiescent period, following which the boat goes over with a lurch."

"And the time when the boat takes that sudden lurch?"

"Last night it was about four hours after high tide."

Judge Newark's eyes sparkled with interest.

Mason said, "Lots of lawyers don't like circumstantial evidence. I do. I've never had any quarrel with the evidence of circumstances. My quarrel is with the habit of giving events the obvious, careless interpretation. I dislike sloppy thinking.

"Take for instance in the present case. We know now that Mrs. Milfield was aboard that yacht at around nine-thirty in the evening. We know that the yacht had tilted pretty well over by that time. We know that the force of

225

water running out would cause the boat to tilt over so that the right or starboard side would be low. We know that someone lit a fresh candle at about the time the yacht was tilted over at an angle of seventeen degrees from the perpendicular. We know that candle was pressed down in a blob of wax that had been left from an earlier candle that had been placed in the same position."

"Then do you think that Mrs. Milfield committed the crime?" Judge Newark asked. "If so, how? Bear in mind the medical testimony that the blow must have been a powerful one."

"So," Mason said cheerfully, "we're faced with an apparent contradiction. The murder must have been committed when the yacht was on an even keel, otherwise that bloodstained footprint wouldn't have been in the exact center of the tread on the companionway, yet if the body rolled down into what I have referred to on this diagram of mine as position number two, death must have occurred within a period of some twenty minutes before the boat took its last heavy list over to starboard."

"You can't reconcile those facts," Burger said. "You'll have to tie your solution to either one or the other. You can't use both."

Mason grinned. "The thing is so simple it slips right through your fingers."

"I'm afraid I don't follow you," Burger said with offended dignity.

Mason said, "The man was killed and the body originally fell in position number two. The *murderer* rolled it back to position number one and then after a while the tide rolled it back again to position number two. But by that time the hemorrhage had stopped. Simply because we found bloodstained carpet under the head of the body when it was lying in position number two, we jumped to the conclusion that there must have been a hemorrhage when the tide rolled the body into that position. The other explanation is so simple and so obvious that it makes you mad you didn't think of it right at the start."

Judge Newark took Mason's diagram. Hamilton Burger got up to walk around behind the judge's desk, and peered down over his shoulder.

"I'll be damned," Burger said softly under his breath.

"But if the body fell into position number two," Judge Newark pointed out, "then the man didn't meet his death by striking his head against the edge of the threshold. What *did* cause his death?"

"The heavy iron poker that goes with the wood stove on the yacht."

"Then if the man was struck from behind with a poker," Judge Newark said, "it eliminates the theory of the strong powerful man. Even a woman could have smashed the poker down on Milfield's head with sufficient force to have cracked his skull—if she'd struck him from behind and caught him unawares."

"Exactly," Mason said. "But the murderer overlooked one thing. Why was the body moved to position number one? Obviously because the murderer wanted to implicate Burbank. Once that New Orleans case was dragged into the open, Burbank would have been convicted on prejudice alone.

"So," Mason went on, "the fact that the murderer tried to put Roger Burbank in this spot shows that it must have been someone who knew about Roger Burbank's past."

Mason picked up the diagram, folded it, pushed it back in his pocket, said, "Of course, it's not up to *me* to tell the district attorney's office how to run its business, but if I were Mr. Burger I would certainly start a little third degree. When the murderer moved that body, it was a giveaway. And that, gentlemen, gives you all I know about the case of the crooked candle. It's enough to bring about a solution—if you work fast."

21

■

Mason, Della Street, Carol Burbank, and Roger Burbank sat in Mason's office. Roger Burbank was nervously smoking a cigar. Mason drummed lightly on the desk top. Della Street sat on the edge of her secretarial chair. Carol Burbank alone gave no outward indication of nervous tension.

Mason said, "Paul Drake is on his way up. He just phoned."

Carol said, "Do you think Judge Newark had all this figured out?"

"Not *all* the angles," Mason said. "He had a theory as to the time of the murder, predicated on the state of the tides, but it hadn't occurred to him that the murderer had given himself away by moving the body. He . . . Here comes Paul now."

Drake had hardly knocked on the door of Mason's office before Della Street had it open for him.

Under the impetus of excitement, Drake had lost his habitual drawl.

"You called the turn, Perry," he said without wasting any time on salutations. "They've got the whole picture now."

"Did they get a confession?" Mason asked.

"Not from the main guy. He's sitting tight as a drum. Mrs. Milfield was the one who caved in."

"What did she say?"

"Enough to give Burger a case. Tell me, Perry, how you knew who committed the murder."

Mason said, "The pay-off was the fact that the body was moved from position number two to postion number one. That indicates that the person who moved it must have known about the skeleton in Roger Burbank's closet, and realized that if he could make it seem the crime had been committed by Burbank, and a clumsy attempt had been made to cover up, Burbank wouldn't stand a ghost of a chance.

"There were three outsiders who knew about the secret of Burbank's past. First there was only Mrs. Milfield, then she told her husband and Van Nuys.

"Van Nuys' entire profits in the oil deal were predicated upon Milfield's ability to collect from Burbank. If Burbank could prove fraud they wouldn't get a nickel.

"As I see the picture, because of the fact that an attempt was made to capitalize upon Burbank's past trouble, the murderer had to be either Mrs. Milfield or Van Nuys. I'm inclined to think Van Nuys is the party because it must have been the murderer who planted that bomb, and when he planted it, he did quite a bit of splashing around with the oars. Not as amateurish as Burwell would have been, but certainly not as expert as Mrs. Milfield who knew a good deal about handling a boat.

"However, it's obvious that Mrs. Milfield must have known about her husband's murder shortly after it occurred and must have co-operated with the murderer to build up an alibi. Therefore, I felt that Mrs. Milfield would probably be the weak link in the chain."

"Well, you're right, Perry," Drake said. "When Burbank realized Milfield had been knocking down on him, he ordered Milfield to meet him for a conference aboard the boat. Milfield, in a panic, got in touch with Van Nuys. Milfield didn't know what to do. He was going to try and stall it along some way if possible. But just in case he couldn't, he told Van Nuys Burbank would have to be eliminated before he could do any talking.

"Between them they worked out a nice little murder scheme. Milfield was to rent a boat from Cameron, row out to the yacht, talk with Burbank, try and persuade Burbank it was all a lie and find out just what he knew. Shortly before he went to keep his appointment, Milfield had got Palermo on the telephone. That must have been shortly after Burbank had left Palermo's cabin. Milfield recognized the description of the 'competitive' speculator who had made the five thousand dollar offer. In desperation, he offered Palermo a large sum of money to go out to Burbank's yacht and tell him that he'd made up the story of the knockdown out of whole cloth, having recognized Burbank, and hoping thereby to get a bigger slice of money for himself.

"Van Nuys was to get a folding boat—an idea they'd picked up from seeing Palermo's boat, carry it down to the estuary, launch it at a point where he wouldn't be seen, and then hang around at a safe distance but within sight of the yacht.

"When Milfield left the yacht he was to signal Van Nuys. If he had managed to pacify Burbank, then nothing was to have been done. But if he hadn't been able to save the situation with a lot of convincing lies, backed by Palermo's repudiation of his earlier statement, then Van Nuys was to slip quietly down the estuary, drifting along with the outgoing tide, place a bomb on the deck of the yacht, drift down the channel for a hundred yards or so, then swing around and row back to the place where he'd left his car, collapse his boat and drive back.

"Van Nuys would need an alibi for the time of the explosion.

"So Van Nuys, with whom Mrs. Milfield was really infatuated, worked out this alibi scheme. Mrs. Milfield was to go to the airport at just about the time the explosion was to take place. She was to telephone Burwell in San Francisco, saying she'd decided to join him, but that circumstances beyond her control had changed her mind. Burwell was an infatuated, inexperienced chap who had fallen head over heels in love with Mrs. Milfield. She'd given him a tumble just as a casual flirtation. He had written a lot of impassioned letters asking her to run away with him.

"So Mrs. Milfield worked out this fake note which she was to pretend to leave for her husband, gave Van Nuys the note and the letters Burwell had written her. Van Nuys, under pressure, was to tell very reluctantly about how Mrs. Milfield, the emotional gypsy, had been out at the airport and how he had joined her. He was to substantiate his story by dramatically producing the very note she was supposed to have left for her husband together with the packet of Burwell's letters.

"But Burbank lost his temper, knocked Milfield over and decided to have him arrested. He climbed out to the deck of the yacht, untied Milfield's skiff and cast it adrift, then got in his own dinghy, started the outboard motor and vanished in the direction of the yacht club.

"Naturally, Van Nuys was quite disturbed. He promptly rowed out to the yacht and found Milfield somewhat groggy from a punch on the jaw. And Van Nuys was so completely, utterly angry with Milfield that he lost his own temper, and Milfield in turn lost his, accused Van Nuys of intimacy with his wife, and struck him. Van Nuys was no match for Milfield with his fists. He was knocked over by the first blow but saw the heavy iron poker lying near where he fell. He picked it up and cracked Milfield over the head. The body fell in what you've referred to as position number two.

"When Van Nuys saw that Milfield was dead, he was in a sudden panic. Then it occurred to him that since Burbank had had a fight with Milfield, he could make it appear that Milfield had died as a result of a blow Burbank had struck, and incidentally make it appear that

Burbank was trying to use the same excuse he used before when he had killed a man in New Orleans.

"So Van Nuys rolled the body over to a position directly in front of the brass-covered threshold which led to the inner cabin, opened the door to the inner cabin, and arranged everything so that the crime was framed on Burbank, then he got in his boat and rowed back—but he had to tell Mrs. Milfield.

"That wasn't too difficult. He told her the whole business, told her that if she'd keep quiet he felt certain he could patch up some sort of a settlement on Milfield's oil rights with Burbank, and that Mrs. Milfield would then become a rich widow. Mrs. Milfield had gone to the airport and put through the call to Burwell just as they had planned, leaving it so that police could trace the long distance call as having been placed through one of the booths at the airport. So the alibi that they had fixed up to cover Van Nuys in the murder of Burbank, came in very handy to cover Van Nuys in the murder of Milfield."

Mason said, "I had an idea that alibi might have been cooked up for something else—and I suppose when Mrs. Milfield found out about what had happened she pointed out that Van Nuys had overlooked something."

"That's right," Drake said.

"What was it?"

"A little vest-pocket account book that Milfield kept in code. The Palermo deal wasn't the only one. Milfield had been knocking down in a systematic way, and for his own information he was keeping a little account book which listed his transactions."

"And they decided, I take it, they had to get this book in order to make their claims good against Burbank?"

"That was about the size of it. They knew the police would start trying to pin the murder on Burbank, and felt that once this book was discovered, it wouldn't take the police long to decipher the code, and have a complete record of Milfield's chicanery. This didn't suit Van Nuys or Mrs. Milfield because then Burbank would be able to set aside all of Milfield's contracts on the ground of fraud."

"So Mrs. Milfield volunteered to go and get it, is that right?"

"Right. Burwell had shown up by then, so it was decided Daphne could use her infatuated boy friend to get her out to the yacht. She was confident she could twist him around her finger. No one at the yacht club would know him, and he could rent a boat and row down to the little rickety pier and pick her up. She'd take the boat out to the yacht. Mrs. Milfield felt she was absolutely safe because she could prove she'd been at the airport when the crime was being committed. Well, those are the highlights of the situation. You can see that . . ."

The phone rang.

Mason nodded to Della. She picked up the receiver, listened a moment, then placed her hand over the mouthpiece.

"Chief, there's a blond woman out there with a black eye who says she has to see you at once. Gertie says she's terribly upset and she's afraid she'll have hysterics if . . ."

"Show her into the law library," Mason said. "I'll talk with her there. While I'm doing that, you can get a check from Mr. Burbank payable to Adelaide Kingman for one hundred thousand bucks. You'll excuse me, I know. An hysterical blonde with a black eye would seem to be an emergency case, at least an interesting one—The Case of the Black Eyed Blonde."

Attention Mystery and Suspense Fans

Do you want to complete your collection of mystery and suspense stories by some of your favorite authors? Raymond Chandler, Erle Stanley Gardner, Ed McBain, Cornell Woolrich, among many others, and included in Ballantine's new Mystery Brochure.

For your FREE Mystery Brochure, fill in the coupon below and mail it to: